Wing of the Raven

Wing of the Raven

A Novel of Vancouver's Heritage

by

Virginia Jones Harper

GODWIN BOOKS

ROBERT STUART THOMSON, EDITOR

VANCOUVER • BRITISH COLUMBIA • CANADA

Wing of the Raven

Copyright © Virginia Jones Harper
Godwin Books, Vancouver, Canada, 1997

ISBN # 0-9696774-5-6

Printed by Hignell Book Printing, Winnipeg,Manitoba
Cover design, text formatting: Sherwood Graphics, Surrey, B.C.

For information write to:

GODWIN BOOKS
P.O. Box 4781, Vancouver, B.C. V6B 4A4

———

*With the exception of historically prominent persons
identified as such, the characters of this novel
are entirely fictitious.*

———

Canadian Cataloguing in Publication Data:

HARPER, VIRGINIA JONES
Wing of the Raven

I Title.

PS8565.A6427W56   1997   C813'.54
PR9199.3.H37W56   1997

With love to:

Martha, Rob, and Leah
Melissa and John
Angela, Tess, Gregory, Sara, and Marisa
Danielle, Stephan, and Robert

Acknowledgements

*In preparation of this novel, the author
is grateful to her husband for his unwavering support,
and to the following persons for their generous
and valuable help:*

MR. TED STAUNTON,
graphic artist and author of a coming novel, *The Seventh Magpie*

MR. JOHN E. (TED) ROBERTS, of Victoria, B.C.,
an authority on the life of Captain George Vancouver
and author of *A Discovery Journal.*

MR. FRANCIS MANSBRIDGE,
Curator of the North Vancouver Archives

Staff members of
THE VANCOUVER PUBLIC LIBRARY,
THE CITY OF VANCOUVER ARCHIVES,
and the
NORTH VANCOUVER DISTRICT AND CITY LIBRARIES

JUDITH G. KELLEY
and
GEOFFREY P. KELLEY,
Member National Assembly, Province of Quebec.

Contents

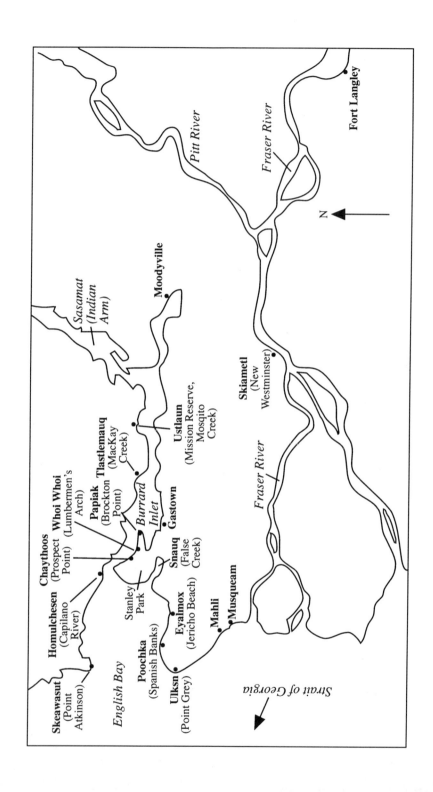

Introduction

This is a tale of Vancouver, not of the majestic, glittering city of today but of the people who occupied its beaches and woodlands before today – the people who planted and nurtured its roots.

Early man was first. Many scientists believe that he traversed the Bering Land Bridge from Siberia when the most recent Ice Age dropped the sea level and exposed the bridge. Then man migrated from the barren Arctic into present North America, populating the British Columbia area about 7050 B.C. After that, some Salish Indians left inland plateaus, crossed the Coastal Mountains, and absorbed coastal cultures into thir own, becoming known as Coast Salish Indians. Most researchers agree that early man probably did not resist the Indian influx. However, mystery shrouds knowledge of the coastal Indians before the late eighteenth century, because they passed down their history only vocally and pictographically.

Some Coast Salish, the Squamish, settled at the head of Howe Sound with fishing camps and additional villages on the north shore of Burrard Inlet. Another group, the Stalo, occupied the lower Fraser River valley. The Musqueam, a Stalo division, centred their villages where the river flowed into the Strait of Georgia, and some Musqueam went around the "battle ground of the west wind" at Ulksn (Point Grey) to establish themselves in English Bay and on the south shore of Burrard Inlet.

The Squamish and Musqueam probably lived together in Burrard Inlet in relative peace – intermarrying, and sharing fishing waters and hunting terrain. Together they settled shores that in time would attract men of varied tongues – explorers, fur-traders, colonists, and gold-miners – shores that would become the waterfront city of Vancouver.

PART I

The Heritage

CHAPTER I

Wakening placidly on her reed sleeping mat, Kah-te stretched one slim leg and then the other. Her fingers dangled on the gravelly earth floor.

Consciousness came all at once, and abruptly she stilled herself. She squinted, ready to feign sleep if she saw her master, Kwamu; for surely he would be on her, his heavy body pressing on her and his distasteful man-thing hurting her again.

A dim, grey dawn silhouetted the open door at the front corner of the plank-walled longhouse and filtered wispily through chinks and smoke vents.

With the other slaves Kah-te slept in the rear of the room; but she could make out the forms of Kwamu and one of his wives, who dozed feet-to-feet on a platform extending around the walls.

When she decided, with relief, that Kwamu was asleep, she opened her eyes fully and focused momentarily on his young son Luhk. She listened to the muted sounds of early morning: a baby fussing in its cradle, a crow hopping on the roof, black-capped chickadees twittering in shrubs beside the house, and a small dog sniffing at a fire pit. She heard an occasional snore from sections of the platform ccupied by Kwamu's relatives. At the sound of heavy breathing and a muffled groan, she knew without turning her head that Kwamu's brother was coming together with one of his wives; amused, she watched his sprawled hunting dog thump its tail supportively, eyes fastened on its master.

Paw-neset, the old *si'la* [grandfather], rose from the platform, garmented himself, streaked his face with red ochre, and smeared his body with insect-repelling bear grease. Then he crossed to Luhk's mat and nudged him with steely fingers.

As Kah-te watched, Luhk staggered to his feet and steadied himself. Yawning, he brushed one fist across his face. He was naked, customary for youths except in moons of stinging winds, and Kah-te noticed how his body had matured since winter. He had typical Musqueam features – dark eyes, coppery skin, and short build. His black hair, hanging shoulder-length, was shiny from rinses in eulachon oil and urine. To his people, his attractive features were his wide face and slanting forehead, deformed by his parents as a privilege of rank when he was an infant.

Kah-te saw Luhk glance at her, then turn and duck through the low door. She napped again, for soon Kwamu's wives would be ordering chores for her.

2

Paw-neset led the way across the clearing of the Musqueam village, Mahli, to a copse of alders, then down a steep, bracken-lined path to the north bank of the river that one day would be named the Fraser. He and Luhk joined other adolescent boys with their trainers, usually grandfathers, who gathered each dawn for a ritual designed to condition the boys' lean bodies.

"Other sun-ups you dived and bit stones. Now, switches!" ordered Paw-neset, handing Luhk a bundle of hemlock cuttings. "Rub in spirit of the evergreen!"

Plunging into shallows of the river, Luhk found footing on the slick, muddy bottom. When a boy near him complained about the cold water, Luhk said, "I don't mind. My elders put me in the river before I could walk. And this moon, there's no more floating ice! River will be warm 'til spirit sends frost again." He cringed because the switches were harsh, but he vigorously stroked his skin with them; his *si'la* accepted no excuses.

The year was 1791, mid-July by white peoples' calendar. To the Pacific Northwest native it was the first lunar division of the year, the beginning of the *tsukai* [sockeye salmon] run from the Pacific Ocean to beds far upstream in the Fraser River tributaries, where the fish would spawn and die. The prized, red fleshed *tsukai* was the year-round mainstay of his diet, and this year was the one-in-every-four when there would be a major run.

Excitedly Luhk looked across the river to fishing camps on the south bank, camps of friendly people whom white men would classify as Coast Salish. Many fish, he reflected. My family will need me. Maybe my *si'la* . . . .

"Rub!" Paw-neset shouted. "Are you soft like a squid, weak like a girl?" He was kind but demanding, feeling a need to control the supernatural power that Luhk possessed at puberty.

Paw-neset stood majestically on the riverbank. His lined face was scarred from smallpox. He had knotted his straggly hair with a deerskin thong and adorned his chest with rank-befitting bone and shell necklaces. His breechclout of tanned buckskin hung from a braided belt – long enough to draw through his legs and fasten at the back when he was working. His feet were bare.

Paw-neset's gruff manner belied the love he felt for Luhk. He exulted in his descent from Seleeptim, First Man of the Musqueam; and in being the elder of an important family and tutor of his pubescent grandsons. As a *si'la*, his role was to rear the children, freeing parents for other tasks, and to teach the myths and legends of his people. Luhk was qualified, he convinced himself, to succeed Kwamu, his father, as the *sia'm* [village leader].

Signalling Luhk, Paw-neset trod soundlessly along the pebbly bank. He passed some decaying rubbish, a row of mat-covered dugout canoes, a mound of cockle shells, and a contrivance of woven willow for trapping ducks on foggy nights.

Shivering slightly, Luhk jogged behind. Gulls soared above them, shrieking delight in the abundance of fish; swallows hawked for insects, and a bald eagle scanned prey from a tall birch. Two canoes glided past, a trawl net billowing between them.

When Paw-neset was beyond hearing of other persons at the river, he seated himself on a thick butt of driftwood. Luhk sank to the sand beside him, characteristically resting on his haunches with chin on his knees. Both were still, their way of pondering words before speaking.

Paw-neset broke the reverie. "You are brave, my grandson," he said, "and humble about your rank. You can wrestle, hunt with bow, fish with spear and net, and paddle with steady stroke. You know that all creatures are your ancestors, and that man and animal have different covers but are equal. You know the eagle is lord in the air, the whale in the sea, and the wolf on land."

After pausing a moment, Paw-neset went on, looking directly at Luhk. "Boy sounds leave your throat, and your man seeds ripen. One more thing for you to be a man."

Luhk jerked his head in alarm. For suddenly he feared what his *si'la* was about to say. It must be time for his *kwakwaiyiset*, when he would seek his guardian spirit – the ordeal that boys dreaded! He had not expected it so soon. But he pretended to be calm. To show fright would be cowardly, and he wished to arouse neither the anger nor the contempt of his grandfather.

Paw-neset detected the fleeting look of terror. "This moon is the time," he continued. "Before you become unclean with woman and animals catch that scent. Go deep in the forest. I'll tell you what direction. Stay 'til animal spirit speaks to you!"

"I . . . I don't know . . . what to do," stammered Luhk. The prospect of contacting a spirit horrified him, but he knew he must, if he wished to become a *sia'm*.

"Dig wild onion and swallow it, then don't eat or sleep. Bleed your legs. Dig a cave, heat a rock, and sweat. Find a black stone and rub your nipples with it to force out old life. When you're weak, your vision will come. In a trance."

"Trance? . . . in a trance?"

"Or a dream. Your *sulia* [guardian spirit] will enter you, bc part of you. You will hear an animal call."

"If I hear many animals, how do I know which?"

"By a special sign . . . maybe a thunderbird feather or that of a grouse."

Luhk thought for a moment. "Spirit will show my dance?" he asked.

"Ay, show your dance, how to paint your face and be your animal." His tone softening, Paw-neset added, "And your song."

"My song," repeated Luhk with elation.

"Your sulia will serve you and always be with you. Always. 'Til you become old and lose your *siwcn* [power]."

Paw-neset ignored the question in Luhk's raised eyes. "I warn of danger," he said.

Luhk drew in his breath, waiting.

"Your *sulia* will give you fright. Your heart will pound. You will heave with vomit, quake as when the earth trembles. But you will not run. You will be still like a rock. You will let your sulia possess you but not know your fear." Leaning forward, he lowered his voice threateningly. "Spirits will punish if you speak of your *kwakwaiyiset*. Dangerous to show your song, dance, or *sulia* 'til winter dance time. Do not tell anyone if you will be a shaman, warrior, or teller of tales. . . ."

"But I want to carve masks like you . . . or be a hunter

like my father!"

"Your guardian *sulia* will choose."

Luhk was silent. Then he asked, "When do I go?"

"Before the sun sinks."

"I'll miss the *tsukai!*"

"You'll be more useful as a real man. As . . . as a fighter. Your father, our *sia'm,* wants fighters."

"You mean the Euclataw . . . there'll be a raid?"

The Euclataw! Mere mention of that hostile Kwakiutl people struck terror in the Coast Salish! In summer, when allies banded together at the river, they could defend each other; but that did not deter the warring Euclataw, who swooped upon them occasionally in sixty-foot battle canoes to murder, plunder, and take slaves. Luhk shuddered, thinking of the most recent raid, twenty moons before, when the Euclataw massacred many Mahli persons and took his sister as a captive.

"Ay, there's a rumor," replied Paw-neset. "Eagle, spirit of your father, is angry because Mahli does not attack the Euclataw!"

"*We* raid *them?*" Luhk's eyes went wide.

Paw-neset raised a hand. "My grandson," he said, his voice tinged with sadness, "The Euclataw, not the Musqueam, make war. They made war with our grandsires."

Luhk sensed the sadness. "You don't want a raid."

"When freshet washes away dam, the beaver does not try to be powerful like the flood. He rebuilds dam, forgets freshet."

Waiting for Luhk to grasp his meaning, Paw-neset rose and faced the river, rosy with a tint of the rising sun. "Enough!" he said. "Dawn is gone and our people stir!" He placed one hand squarely on Luhk's arm with a reassuring squeeze.

3

Musqueam villages dotted the river estuary and its network of bogs and creek mouths. Mahli was closest to the sea, perched on a bluff above reach of spring thaws. About five hundred persons lived in Mahli and a neighbouring settlement that bore the name of the people: Musqueam.

The Musqueam society was spiritual, with belief in Qals, the Great Transformer and most powerful spirit. The villages consolidated in times of trouble, but each was a political entity, controlled by one family that theoretically elected its *sia'm* but passed the position hereditarily.

At Mahli, Kwamu's family included blood relatives for several generations. They lived in the centre longhouse of abutting post-and-beam units with one single-pitched roof. Unimportant relatives – considered degraded because they lacked children or supernatural power – occupied end sections.

Kwamu resided with his favourite wife and their children, of whom Luhk was the eldest; two other wives and his children by each were on either side. He kindled the wives' jealousy by frequenting their quarters at his pleasure. Others in the house included his brothers and their families, Pawneset and his wives, a mother-in-law, and the slaves.

Each family unit used a fire pit, part of the sleeping platform, and storage space for its wood and baskets of food, tools, and other possessions. Racks of dried fish hung from ceiling beams. As a wealthy man, Kwamu also owned two carved cedar boxes filled with furs, skins, and blankets.

Kwamu's communal household respected him. Though he was more father figure than absolute ruler, his house was the seat of the local government; and though he shared some decision-making, villagers generally regarded his word as law.

Returning to the house, Paw-neset handed Luhk a breechclout on a waist thong. "Cover yourself now, like a man," he said. After Luhk awkwardly fastened it over one hip, slid it forward, then darted from the house, Paw-neset smiled with satisfaction.

CHAPTER II

"Kah-te! Kah-te!" Luhk cried the name urgently as he hurried around the house. His people addressed others with terms of relationship such as "my son" or "my *si'la*," but they called a slave by name.

He found Kah-te bent over a deerskin. She was scraping it with a stone flesher and concentrating to avoid puncturing it. She paused frequently to rinse the blade in a basket of brackish water or to wipe splatter from her face.

"Kah-te!" Luhk seethed to spill his turbulent thoughts. She was the only person in whom he confided.

Kah-te straightened and raised her head. Her back and breasts glistened with sweat. Noting the addition of Luhk's breechclout, she instinctively tugged at her brief apron, the uniform garment of a slave.

"At sundown I go!" cried Luhk.

"Go? Go where?"

"To . . . to find my spirit!"

Tossing her head to acknowledge the importance of his words, Kah-te smiled. "Ah," she said softly, "then you'll be a man."

"Kah-te, I . . . I'm afraid!"

"You've waited many moons for this!"

"To be a man and take care of you!"

"My master, your father, takes care of me."

"I don't want you to be a slave. I want to raise your rank."

"You speak man words," said Kah-te. Then she sighed. "You are noble, I am slave. It will ever be."

"No! I'll get many blankets and make a big *klanak* [feast]. I'll tell about you and give you a name to wash away the stain of being a slave! Then I . . ."

Kah-te's laugh interrupted Luhk. "Then?" She laughed

again, a bit derisively, at the plan she considered ridiculous.

But Luhk did not laugh. "Then I'll marry you!"

Kah-te sobered, startled by his mature behaviour. "You are kind, son of my master," she said. "But you are to be *sia'm*. Forget me." Reaching for a wooden frame, she began to lace the skin to it rapidly, as if to erase such talk of freedom.

Surging with power she attributed to being a woman, Kah-te was strong-willed, but she had resigned herself to slave status. To her knowledge, there was no ransom attempt after Kwamu bartered for her, and she knew not whether she was born in slavery or captured as an infant. She was content because there was no escape; to her there was no need for discussion.

Luhk struggled for words that would not come. He almost forgot his dilemma. "Kah-te, you and I – we're closer than family."

"We're friends."

"We will marry!"

Kah-te lowered the lacing awl and looked straight at Luhk. "You are fourteen winter-to-winters. I am . . . much older!"

"You don't know!"

"I know how many moons I have been a woman."

Sighing, Kah-te wished that Kwamu were less aware of her womanhood, for she dared not object to his sexual demands. As punishment he could cut her kneecaps to cripple her, or he could sell her to a master who might be worse. But she conceded that he did not mistreat her. Her fear was of bearing his child, for which he probably would have her put to death; she appealed to the shaman regularly for preventive herbs.

She did not understand Kwamu's desire for her because, as a slave, she must short-crop her hair and was denied the head flattening that would make her more attractive. Her forehead was so normally rounded that Kwamu called her "dog head." Her skin was tanned by the sun, her legs moved in natural strides, and her breasts were too full to be desirable. She despaired of her looks and reasoned that Kwamu took her without noticing them.

As her thoughts raced, Kah-te worked faster. She finished lacing the pelt and applied deer brains to soften it for sewing.

Luhk watched in a silence of frustration. He wanted to talk of his coming ordeal and his fear. "Kah-te, I . . ."

One of Kwamu's wives limped to them, wincing from gashes on her feet that Kwamu made when he suspected her of infidelity. She wore a sleeved smock, fastened with bone pins to an underskirt. "Enough prattle," she said flatly. "Girl, draw some water, heat the cooking stones." Turning to Luhk, she added, "Son of my husband from another womb, your *si'la* said you're to go to the sweat house!" Her manner was lustreless, yet authoritative. Like all Musqueam wives, she obeyed her husband and accepted her subservience; yet she believed that women, more than men, are connected to earth and share its energy.

Luhk darted a frantic look at Kah-te. Then he pushed through a patch of fireweed to the sweat house.

2

Bent maple saplings covered with earth and bark formed the dome-shaped sweat house. Moistened leaves lined the interior. A fire smouldered outside the door.

Luhk tossed three stones on the fire, waited until they were white-hot, then carried them inside on flattened sticks to a hole in the floor. He closed the door and sprinkled the stones with water to cloud the room with steam.

Shedding his clout, he crouched low, contemplating his *kwakwaiyiset* and his grandfather's mention of a raid. He also pondered the stirring within him when he was near Kah-te or thought of her. Strangely, he told himself, I don't mind her plain head, but I know her rank will matter when I become *sia'm,* because my people will *make* it matter! I don't understand.

Kwamu jerked open the door, startling Luhk. "To the water!" he boomed. He was broadshouldered with a muscular chest. His hair fell unbound, and he had painted his face and belted his calf length shirt with cedar rope. To Luhk, he seemed to fill the doorway with his might.

Obediently, Luhk ran from the hut and plunged into the river, his overheated body twitching with shock. Later, at the longhouse, he quietly watched Kah-te lift baked wapato roots from the ashes and chunks of deer from sticks above the coals. Another slave put out steamed salmon, oysters, salmonberry shoots, herbs, tenderized camas roots, and pickled acorns.

As Luhk wiped his mouth with a frayed bark square at the end of the meal, his apprehension increased, because his father and grandfather were whispering and glancing at him. His pulse quickened when they came to him.

"Go now," said Kwamu in an assertive tone.

"It's not yet dusk!" Luhk cried. He kicked at a black beetle scampering across the dirt floor.

"Two women here are in menses. Dangerous," Paw-neset explained. "Come. Leave your clout, bring your knife. Shaman waits."

Luhk's throat tightened and his hands were clammy. Gulping, he rose, unfastened his breechclout, and picked up his knife. He followed Paw-neset across a field. Hearing a rumble of thunder, he noticed that clouds were darkening. He jumped nervously when a blue heron flapped from its nest, again when a shaman bounded from weeds at the edge of the woods.

Shaking globular deer-hoof rattles, the shaman leaped forward, his skirt flopping and his red-painted chin bobbing. His mystical power flashed into Luhk's mind – his ability to heal, conduct ceremonies, cause thunderstorms, or induce death and evil.

The shaman thrust his arms upward. "This boy seeks his *sulia* in a *slalakum* [secret] place!" he chanted. "Give him a song!" Then he and Paw-neset left abruptly.

The air was heavy. Except for the croaking of frogs, foreboding rain, there was an eerie quiet. Swallows flew low, songbirds and insects were still, and grasses did not rustle.

Luhk hesitated. Then he turned to the tangle of underbrush and foliage and found a creek flowing from the woods to the river – his path. As the first drops of rain hit the earth, he breathed deeply and warily entered the shadowy unknown.

CHAPTER III

After the last Ice Age, melting glaciers slashed the Coastal Mountains. As the glaciers inched to the Pacific Ocean, they gouged canyons and carved a serpentine shoreline. One mammoth, gravel-tinged glacier furrowed a channel thirty miles wide, creating the mainland of present British Columbia and many mountainous islands, of which Vancouver Island was the largest. That channel, an arm of the Pacific Ocean, later was known as the Strait of Georgia. The Fraser River flowed into it.

Several miles north of the Fraser River, a finger of the strait squeezed into an inlet through a slim entrance known as the Narrows. At the Narrows another river, the Homulcheson [later, Capilano], catapulted powerfully from mountains into a deep canyon and entered the inlet at the Squamish *okwumuq* [village] of Homulchesen.

Near Homulchesen, at the *okwumuq* of Tlastlemauq, Tahulet morosely sat behind a partition in her father's longhouse and twined a rush basket. She was in isolation because she exuded supernatural power during her initial menstrual period. Sight of her would drive away game, and her touch would contaminate a weapon. Sighing, she rose and peeped through a slit in the wall.

Sunbeams flickered in a breeze that stirred massive firs and cedars near the house. To Tahulet the rays seemed to beckon where she could not go. Looking up at the humpbacked foothills and the Mountain of the Grouse, which towered behind Tlastlemauq, she sighed again. She longed for the carefree childhood that now was behind her.

She recalled a conversation with her mother while they split cedar bark to make *slowi* for blankets. Usually timid, she had asserted herself that day. "Dull," she complained.

"A rich husband wants many skills in a wife," her

mother had replied. "A husband wants a work partner. You should be fit to marry the son of a *sia'm*."

"My mother, it's not yet time for me to marry!"

"Soon you'll be a woman."

Following her mother's gaze, Tahulet flushed and glanced down at the pointed breasts showing under her smock, developing despite daily rubbing with smooth stones.

Remembering that day, Tahulet's lip trembled. Atsaian, her father, was *sia'm* of Tlastlemauq; he expected her to marry well and guard his social position with unblemished behaviour. At twelve she neither understood changes in her body nor recognized her blossoming beauty.

To her people, Tahulet's beauty suited her rank. As the child of a *sia'm,* in her infancy she received the same cranial deformation as had the Musqueam boy Luhk: pinched nose, sloped forehead, and bulging cheeks. Her hair glistened from urine rinses; and her skin, rarely exposed to the sun, was fashionably light. Her parents had reshaped her legs with tight bands around her ankles, forming desirable indentations as her body grew.

An elderly attendant bathed Tahulet daily and massaged her body with brambles, a procedure believed to improve intelligence. She braided goat wool into Tahulet's hair and smoothed her eyebrows with saliva.

Each day the shaman danced into the room and Tahulet cowered. *"Sinalke,"* he droned, "make this girl pure!" He painted her face and fed her a piece of salmon. At dusk he removed the paint at the creek, apologizing to fish for tainting the water.

On the day the shaman produced thorn needles, Tahulet whimpered in dread of the procedure that would follow. He tattooed four rows of dots on her ankles and wrists and rubbed in sooty alder ashes. Then, while the attendant gripped her head, he plucked edges of her face to raise her hairline – another privilege of aristocracy.

"Much beauty you have. An important *sia'm* will want you for a wife," soothed the attendant, as she wiped Tahulet's tears and quieted her sobs.

On the eighth evening, a *sqomten* came. Tahulet shivered as he pranced about her, jiggling his rattles. A *sqomten*, she knew, was a medicine-man and had more power than a shaman. He oiled her hair and dressed her in a knee-length deerskin shroud, the mark of a high-ranking, mature woman. Then, with a flourish, he backed from the enclosure.

Slaves removed the partitions from around Tahulet, and she blinked in surprise. One hundred relatives and guests filled the longhouse, leaving clear only a centre area for the dancers. For her *heisut* – celebration of womanhood – Atsaian had "called the people as witnesses" and exhilarated them with oollaly-berry drinks until they churned to express themselves spiritually. Seeing Tahulet, they began to drum with sticks.

The dancers! Tahulet cringed at the inhuman eyes and beaked noses of their masks when they charged into the room and swooped over her body for *me'kwn,* the cleansing ritual. Their chants terrified her. Working into a trance, they circled until dawn, then feasted with family and guests.

Afterward, everyone slept, some on the wall platform, others at the fires. Tahulet moved her mat to a quiet corner and thought about the demands of maturity.

"We'll have stories tonight before the dance," Atsaian said the second evening. "I'll save a special tale I have for last." Then he handed wooden tally sticks to a man who volunteered to talk first. "Divide your story," he ordered. "Turn the sticks as you go."

For three nights the guests repeated timeworn Squamish legends, of which no one ever tired, because they represented history, and keeping them alive was vital. Women wailed and men quivered with emotion at several of the fables.

"We Squamish had three catastrophes," a speaker said. "One was a flood. Great Spirit made Kalana, our First Man, all-human and gave him three things man needs: a wife, an adze, and a salmon trap. After Kalana died, the people became wicked, so Spirit caused rivers to flood. Flood lasted sixty sun-to-suns."

"Did everyone drown?"

"All except Kalana's son Cheatmuh. With his wife Cheatmuh landed his canoe on a mountain, the same mountain we see poke in the clouds and sometimes spit smoke. Great White Watcher [Mount Baker]. Cheatmuh filled the earth with offspring."

"You said three catastrophes. The flood was one."

"Ay, two others. The people sinned again and Spirit sent a great snow to punish them. One man, one woman were saved. The third catastrophe was pox. Two lived."

Another speaker gathered the sticks and began a tale of the mallard duck, but a pounding of boards ended the stories. The dancers were impatient!

On the fourth night, Atsaian's brother Nahu talked. "Qais, Great Transformer, took the form of four brothers in a big canoe," he said. "Qais gave wicked man four legs and made the first animal."

The next morning, after most men and boys enjoyed ball games in a meadow, Atsaian lifted Tahulet to an elevated platform outside the house and stood beside her. Dressed ceremoniously, he was ready to assert his wealth and prestige by distributing blankets. He had greased his skin and sprinkled it with particles of mica, so that he glimmered from head to foot. His teeth gleamed pure white. He wore leggings and moccasins fastened at his ankles; a shirt of copper, hammered cloth-thin; a doeskin waistband trimmed with duck feathers; a geometrically-patterned blanket tossed over one shoulder; and a conical hat woven of feathers. Strong and swarthy, he had an authoritative look.

"My daughter is marriage age. These blankets are in her name!" Atsaian shouted, pointing to Tahulet as he tossed blanket after blanket, all the while making sure each guest received an amount comparable to his rank. He dropped torn strips to the poor, whom he considered unworthy of more.

Maybe they will take blankets but not want to marry me, Tahulet said to herself. She tried to crouch where no one could see her.

"I'll give a *klanak* when my daughter marries!" Atsaian added. "That day should be soon, after I am so generous today!" Then he stilled the drums and vigorously shook a rattle until he hushed his audience. "My people, I tell you a big thing," he declared. "We Squamish are to get the Musqueam *whoi whoi* [mask]!"

Even Tahulet gasped in wonder.

"The great *Sxwaixwe* mask of the Musqueam?"

"Ay, the great *Sxwaixwe.*" To quiet the buzz of incredulousness Atsaian again shook the rattle, its fringe jumping. "I, Atsaian, promise a wedding with the *Sxwaixwe!* Musqueam marriages are grander than ours! Their death and puberty rites, too. The *Sxwaixwe* mask is better."

Atsaian stopped for effect, then continued: "I swear our dancers will wear the *Sxwaixwe* when my daughter weds!" His voice rose to a dramatic pitch. "May *Sinalke* strike me if I fail!" With a bow he stepped into the house, leaving his guests subdued.

2

After the guests departed, Atsaian returned to the house front, where villagers usually met to conduct business or to gossip in leisure hours. They waited for him that day. With women and children, Tahulet sat cross-legged on the grass.

"How, *Sia'm?* How will you get the mask?" a man asked. "The Musqueam First Man received it from a spirit. The *Sxwaixwe* is theirs, not ours!"

"No, no," argued another. "A figure wearing the mask appeared when a Musqueam man was at a lake seeking his spirit."

"The Musqueam got the mask upriver!"

"No, a man caught it on a fish line in this inlet!"

"Wait!" interrupted Atsaian. "All those tales are recent. Our supreme tyee, Te Kiapilanoq, agrees."

"Recent? Why recent?"

"Because the Musqueam have had the *Sxwaixwe* only several winter-to-winters! I know . . . I asked their *si'las!*"

"Then where did the Musqueam get the *Sxwaixwe?*"

"Aha! That's the story I promised! A true story! As I heard it from Paw-neset, an old Mahli *si'la.*"

Atsaian was an *iagoo* [story-teller]. As the men hushed and squatted comfortably to listen, he placed the tally sticks on a board. Turning them one by one and embellishing his words with hand motions, he recited the story:

Upriver from the Musqueam lived a young man ill with q'm [leprosy]. His putrid skin fell off. There was no cure. His people sent him to die in a cave. But he fell off a cliff into a lake. As he sank, an old man caught him and took him to a house on the lake bottom. Many sick people were there.

"Cure these people," the old man ordered. "They have sores

from human spit on the lake."

"Only if you cure me," replied the young man with qum.

The old man rubbed the young man with bark and cured him. Then the young man healed the others with the same bark. The people offered blankets as pay. The young man shook his head and said, "I want that Sxwaixwe!" He pointed to a mask and costume spread on a bench.

"Return home," replied the grateful people. "In one moon Beaver will make a tunnel from this lake to your river. He also will make a deep pool. You fish there. Sxwaixwe will come."

At the proper time the young man dropped a line in the special pool. His sister was with him. When they felt a jerk on the line, they tugged. They heard a noise. The old man from the lake poked through some reeds. He wore the Sxwaixwe mask and costume.

The old man showed dances and chants. He took off the mask and costume and gave them to the young man. "Guard these well, use wisely," he warned. "Use to celebrate when a daughter becomes a woman and when a couple sits on a pile of blankets to marry. Also at death. Beware of supernatural power!" Then he added, "This mask is thunder, but I give you power to carve others."

Then a black cloud darkened the sky and thunder boomed. The old man disappeared.

The young man put the Sxwaixwe in a basket and hung it in a tree. It stayed there many moons, until the sister married and moved downriver. She took a copy of the mask. Her daughter married a Musqueam and moved the mask there. It's been there to this day!

3

At the end of his narrative Atsaian raised his arms. "Soon the *Sxwaixwe* will come to the Squamish!" he cried.

He put down the last tally stick, which meant that other men could talk.

"How will you get the *Sxwaixwe?*" the men again asked.

"You'll see. Later," replied Atsaian. "We go to the river of the Musqueam in four sun-to-suns. The *tsukai* are running, and berries are ready."

"The *tsawin* [coho] swarms here!" cried Nahu, pointing to the Homulchesen River. "Isn't that enough for you?"

Unlike the navigable lower Fraser River, the Homulchesen was a rapid mountain torrent, but it also was a major salmon spawning ground. Nahu's question was valid.

"My brother," Atsaian answered, "the *tsukai* is best, but it swims in the river of the Musqueam, not here. For the best we go there. It's also important to be with other peoples."

Then Nahu shouted, "This inlet is safe for us! Sayn Uskih the serpent guards us, with his head at Papiak [Brockton Point], and his tail in the channel. The Euclataw are afraid to come here. At the river of the Musqueam we're at the Euclataw's mercy!"

"Ay, risky," agreed Atsaian. "But more risky here."

"What risk? Fish, game, and berries are here. Peace, too," argued Nahu. "You are the only one not satisfied, my brother. You . . ."

Two guards rushed into the clearing.

A Euclataw raid? Men leaped to their feet in alarm. Women clutched their children.

"Wait! Hear them!" cried Atsaian.

"An *A'lia* [prophet]!" said one of the men, pointing to a stranger who was following them. "He brings a message. He says men will come with . . . with *white skin!*"

Atsaian sent a slave to fetch the shaman, then stepped

forward, lifting an arm in greeting. *"Kla-how-ya,"* he said.

The stranger's paint was like that of peoples to the south. He carried an iron hoop and a curved flint knife.

"Kla-how-ya," the *A'lia* replied. He and Atsaian spoke in the intertribal jargon that native peoples with different languages had developed centuries before for communication in trading. "I come to warn you," he said forebodingly.

"Warn us? Of what?" Agitation muffled Atsaian's voice.

The stranger spaced his words dramatically: "A black shadow will cover the land, never to pass! A shadow as black as the forest, as black . . . *as black as the wing of the raven!"*

Wing of the raven! Raven, the trickster who could take many forms. Raven, who sometimes posed as Creator of the universe. Raven, who brought light to the world by tossing the sun into the sky from his beak. Powerful, awesome Raven! Why did the *A'lia* compare the shadow to Raven? The prediction was ominous!

"Black shadow?" queried Atsaian, staring blankly.

"Mamathni will come – men in a house moving on water," the *A'lia* went on. "Men with light beards, skin like snow. Called whiteman. They will bring riches like this!" He held up his hoop and knife.

"A spirit?" asked Nahu.

"Whiteman says his spirit is a great *sia'm* in the sky – He Who Dwells Above. He makes the sign of a cross for his spirit."

"If whiteman brings riches, why a black shadow?"

The prophet's face was grave. "Black shadow of evil. Evil riches," he muttered.

Atsaian fidgeted. Then he whispered to a slave, who brought a musket from the house. Holding out the gun, Atsaian said, "I have a magic stick. I traded for it with people who had a hoop like yours. It came on their beach, they said."

The *A'lia* nodded. "Ay, current carried it across the sea."

Then he pointed to the musket, guessing that Atsaian did not comprehend its use. Solemnly, he said, "Magic stick needs balls. Balls kill. Magic stick, balls – evil."

Not understanding, Atsaian put down his gun.

Then the *A'lia* said, "Whiteman is in the North. Soon he'll be everywhere. He brings evil. More pox, too. And he doesn't call us Squamish, Musqueam, or Cowichan. He calls us all *Indian*."

The questions continued.

"Will whiteman bring war like the Euclataw?"

"Something worse than war," replied the prophet. "Whiteman will bring magic sticks like yours, iron like the hoop, but no war. He wants pelts."

"Only pelts for hoops and magic sticks?" Atsaian shook his head and the other men looked baffled. What could be wrong with magic sticks and riches, they wondered, if they did not mean war?

"When will whiteman come?"

"He's already in your waters!"

Eager to move to the next *okwumuq*, the *A'lia* started to his canoe, and Atsaian paid him with a blanket.

While the people were absorbing the prediction, the shaman stepped forward. He had listened intently. Trying to be more impressive than the *A'lia*, he repeated the message but made it worse. Scowling, he cried, "Whiteman will sadden us. Doom!"

The villagers were bewildered. They had not expected the shaman to agree with the prophet's frightening words! For generations, only an occasional attack had disturbed their tranquil existence. Life was orderly, with no pressure of time and few threatening situations. They stirred uneasily.

"Come, my daughter," Tahulet's mother said, leading her into the house. "We won't fear whiteman. Our spirit will protect us. Soon the men will forget what the *A'lia* said. You forget."

Then Atsaian rose, dismissing concern as his wife had suggested. Ignoring Nahu, who had questioned his wisdom, he said decisively, "Stay to fish here if you want. On the fourth sun-up most of us will leave for the river of the Musqueam."

CHAPTER IV

Sko-mish-oath, the Squamish called themselves – canoe makers – and Atsaian was master of the skill in Tlastlemauq. He timed departure for the river with his launching a special canoe. On the morning after the *heisut* and the *A'lia's* visit, he hurried to a secluded grove to inspect his handiwork.

Removing a mat covering, he gazed proudly at his fifty-foot canoe, which would carry forty persons. His eyes moved from the cutwater to the stern. Finest on the inlet, he reflected – as fine as the Haida and Euclataw build! Te Kiapilanoq should like it.

For good luck while he carved the canoe, Atsaian had fasted for a week, and he did not lie with his wives. Then he had searched for a perfect cedar.

"Sulia," he had implored, "Tell the cedar I will not waste it. I ask that it not crack! I honour you and the cedar spirit!"

Instead of felling the entire tree, he cut two gashes half around it, the distance between them equalling the proposed length of his canoe. He inserted a pole in the top slit and waited while it worked down and a half-round block broke loose.

Why am I so eager? Atsaian asked himself. I have sons, slaves, wives for my bed, a daughter for marriage, and a spirit. I will please Te Kiapilanoq with the *Sxwaixwe* but also with my canoe.

Atsaian's wives knew he was aggressive, always trying to increase his power and fortune, and they competed for his attention. He chose one wife to help him in the forest.

Atsaian and his wife stripped the block and painstakingly chiselled it. The work was so crucial that neither dared to use a comb; a hair could split the cedar! To spread the hull, they filled it with water and wedged bent saplings into it to straighten and push out the sides.

Atsaian danced and chanted. When he approved the gunwale curve, he braced it and sanded it with salmon roe. Finally, he painted family crests and alerted four nephews – mystically there must be four – to carry the hull without touching it to earth.

2

On a drizzly afternoon before he launched his canoe, Atsaian visited the village of Homulchesen. He beached his dugout and hurried to the longhouse of elderly Te Kiapilanoq. In respect, he bowed low before he squatted beside the tyee.

As supreme tyee, Te Kiapilanoq's authority stemmed directly from Kalana, the First Man. He maintained a home at Homulchesen and one at the Howe Sound Squamish stronghold. He felt harmony with the world. To him the bounty of land and sea was so lavish that his people should want for nothing, nor should they have any temptation to sin.

They spoke of trivialities and the *A'lia's* message.

Then Atsaian was silent, considering his words. "At next sun-up," he began, "I will take the Tlastlemauq people to camp at the river of the Musqueam. I will bring the *Sxwaixwe* after fishing. As I told you one moon back!"

"Strong words you speak, *Sia'm,*" said Te Kiapilanoq. "How will you get the *Sxwaixwe?*"

Atsaian smiled confidently. "Only you will hear my plan, honoured Tyee," he replied, looking around to be sure no one was near. "I will use my daughter," he added in a hushed tone. "Her *heisut* is just finished."

"A marriage trade?"

"Ay. Kwamu, the *sia'm* of Mahli has a son."

The tyee looked concerned. "What does Kwamu gain?" he asked.

"Kwamu needs his son to marry a girl of rank. If his son weds low, the *sia'm* title will pass to a nephew. Few girls have a birth as noble as my daughter's!" Pausing, Atsaian said, "Something else, Tyee."

"Ay?"

"When the Euclataw go to the river of the Musqueam, they attack Mahli first. So Kwamu is going to . . . to raid the Euclataw! He needs help!"

"Help? You promise the help of our braves, too, for the *Sxwaixwe?*" Usually calm, Te Kiapilanoq could not keep surprise from his voice – surprise that Atsaian's scheme was so complex.

"If . . . if you permit." Atsaian trembled slightly when he remembered that Qais punishes selfish thoughts.

Te Kiapilanoq considered the proposal. Then he raised his right hand. "Go, *Sia'm,*" he said, emotion showing in his creased face. "Bring the *Sxwaixwe.* But hold two truths. One: your daughter is easily given, our warriors not."

Atsaian swallowed nervously. "Your second truth?" he asked.

"We Squamish are not greedy. We share our wealth."

Recognizing the words as a warning, possibly as a personal rebuke, Atsaian pushed that thought aside. He had the permission he sought, despite its reservation, and he counted on restoring himself to favour with his new canoe. Rising, he smiled and said, "My tyee, I beg you to watch us leave for the river. I have made a canoe to honour you!" Bowing once more, he departed.

3

A soft sea breeze brushed Tahulet's cheek, as she stood on the beach. Trying to forget the *heisut,* she revelled in the glory of the clear morning. The sea was deep blue, streaked with green. Whitecaps sparkled in the sun like rows of diamonds and vanished in lacy foam at her feet. With each receding wave, tiny crabs dug and minnows thrashed in the tidal trench. A heron posed motionlessly. Villagers and slaves yoked dugouts together and packed them for the move to the river of the Musqueam.

"Ho, it comes!"

Atsaian emerged from the woods. He was about to display his canoe! Like porters with a sultan's chair, the four nephews bore the canoe on waist-level poles and carefully lowered it into the surf. It floated and the crowd cheered!

Atsaian received plaudits with an elaborate flourish. Then he hopped aboard. I must hurry, he told himself, to buck the last trace of flood tide and cross the Narrows on the first of the ebb, ahead of dangerous rips.

Rowers pushed off the dugouts and paddled into the current. In the new canoe, which pulled into lead position, Atsaian ordered his men to keep near the north shore for a short time. Te Kiapilanoq, he hoped, would be watching.

More canoes moved out from Homulchesen and Ustlaun [Mosquito Creek]. The caravan crossed to Chaythoos [Prospect Point] and headed across open water for Pookcha [Spanish Banks], intending to stroke close to land from there. A pod of killer whales romped near the boats, their glossy bodies shimmering, and seals cavorted among offshore rocks.

Mesmerized by roll of the current and rhythmic dips of the oars, Tahulet drowsed in her father's canoe. The warmth of the sun caressed her. Other persons nodded.

Suddenly Atsaian barked an order and oarsmen raised paddles with a start. Waves slapped against the boat, and the other canoes churned in all directions.

"What is it?"

"Only a whale!"

"No, no . . . it's too big!"

"Ay-eee!"

Floating before them was an immense black object shaped like a house! Wings billowed above it like mats the Euclataw used for speed, but these were white and much larger!

"A spirit!"

"Sinalke!"

A woman screamed, "Ay-eee, a serpent!"

"Sayn Uskih followed us!"

"No, no, it's the *mamathni!* The *A'lia* said it would come! Men in a tall house that moves on water!"

"Turn back!"

"Whiteman!"

Men scrambled for bows, clubs, and knives.

Choking back alarm, Atsaian calmed his people and conferred with *sia'ms* who pulled alongside. They watched the object move toward Pookcha and stop there, the wings folding.

"Ay-eee, whiteman has *siwcn,*" cried one *sia'm.*

The ship's longboat and five canoes with Musqueam markings came around the Ulksn point. Natives from surf smelt camps at Eyalmox [Jericho Beach] raised oars in welcome!

When they saw that the Musqueam had met no harm, Atsaian and a few *sia'ms* approached. Perhaps whiteman was not an enemy, they reasoned; perhaps they could trade with whiteman for iron like the *A'lia's* hoop.

4

The Viceroy of Mexico had ordered Lieutenant Commander Don Francisco de Eliza to establish territorial rights for Spain in waters surrounding a settlement known as Nootka Sound on Vancouver Island's west coast. Commander Eliza sailed briefly into the Strait of Georgia, but his companion, Pilot Commander Don Jose Maria Narvaez, went farther north.

On that July morning of 1791, Piloto Narvaez observed mud streaks jutting into the strait from a marshy delta and discovered the Rio Biancho [Fraser River] for Spain. Through a high-powered glass he saw Mahli natives packing dugouts. Apparently, he decided, these Indians are not hostile but merely eager to trade. However, from experience with groups that were friendly at first and later became warlike, he ordered his crew to man the ship's guns while he anchored to secure fresh food from the Indians.

Most of the Indians glided canoes to the ship. They were awed by the strange look of the men at the deck railings.

"Ay-eee," commented a *sia'm,* "No women to do chores!"

"Their skin is not white at all and their hair is dark!" said Atsaian. He did not know that the strangers were Latin-coloured Spaniards with a leader who was Greek by birth!

"Their heads are not flat. They're commoners!"

"They all hold magic sticks like Atsaian's. Why?"

When sailors dropped water casks, Eyalmox natives went ashore to fill them. The Musqueam offered fish, and the Squamish added roots and chunks of deer. Covetously eyeing the muskets, the Indians clapped when the Spaniards lowered copper sheets and barrel hoops to the longboat; they liked whiteman's wares but concluded that he was stupid because he did not know their language.

After the bartering, Narvaez pulled anchor. Probably missing Burrard Inlet, he explored part of Howe Sound, naming it Bocas del Carmelo. Turning about, he headed back to Nootka Sound.

5

Several thousand Indians would throng into the Fraser River to fish in mid-August. Most headed far upstream from the delta to supreme fishing grounds at "the Falls." There the salmon swarmed in a canyon, then leaped surging rapids to return to their spawning grounds. And there, between craggy precipices, each people claimed hereditary fishing rocks and set drying racks on the banks. There, too, the rocks held heat at night, and winds dried salmon so that laborious smoking was unnecessary. Truly, the Indians believed, Sinalke had made the Falls special for them.

Atsaian's plan for his people was to camp temporarily near the river mouth before paddling to the Falls. On the bank opposite Mahli he found a clearing and ordered his men to put up houses, using the planks they had yoked to their canoes. He had nodded to Kwamu during trading with the Spaniards. *After our First Salmon ceremony, I'll meet with him*, he decided. *I must not seem too eager.*

The atmosphere was festive; greeting their brothers, the Salmon People, was a happy ritual. At dusk Atsaian's villagers congregated on the riverbank and readied coals in an open trench. Children ran about excitedly, waving cedar branches.

Like a bride making an entrance, the shaman vaulted to the water. With each leap his skirt flapped and down puffed from his hair. His eyes were almost invisible under blackened brows. "Welcome, Salmon People," he cried, "our brothers with human souls. We will take of you only what we need." He dipped a net into the water and scooped a salmon – the scout, he hoped. He wrapped it in bark with the head pointing upstream. Then he led a procession to the fire where he presented the salmon to his wife, who solemnly cleaned and stretched it on a split stick. He roasted the salmon. Then he flung himself high in the air and came down with legs apart and arms akimbo, his face upturned.

"Qais," he shrilled, "you make a home under the sea for the Salmon People, who send their young so we can have food! Of all their sons the *tsukai* serves us best. We ask for many *tsukai!*"

Atsaian and Nahu made speeches, but they sat down when the shaman cut the salmon. With eyes closed, each person swallowed a small portion of the fish, then shuffled counterclockwise around the fire. To end the rite the shaman scattered bones and entrails into the river, so that parts could return to the sea and be renewed as whole salmon.

CHAPTER V

Kwamu watched activity at Atsaian's camp across the river with mixed emotions. He enjoyed visitors, but in summer he worried that a concentration of people would invite another raid. At the same time, a thrill surged through him as he planned his strike against the Euclataw. To him it was adventure! Revenge!

"We'll stop the Euclataw forever!" he exclaimed to his father as they worked in a lean-to behind the longhouse. On a stone he was grinding mussel shells into arrow points.

Paw-neset was carving a bowl and did not reflect Kwamu's elation. He glanced up but said nothing.

Kwamu took no notice. "The Euclataw will find us fierce and won't come again!" he continued, raising his voice. "We'll burn, loot, take slaves, and make the Euclataw weak. We'll kill, too."

"My son," said Paw-neset gravely, "you'll need warriors."

"Ay, upriver people. The Kwantlen and Katzie."

"The Katzie? They're cowards!"

"But they have fighters. Their chief warrior gave his word."

"People fish now for winter."

"We'll go after the fishing ends."

"One time we raided some upriver people. They won't help!"

Kwamu laughed. "That was to get ransom by capturing some women," he said. "They fear the Euclataw and us. They'll help."

Paw-neset pursed his lips dubiously. "We're happy," he said. "We have peace. Forget revenge! Forgive the Euclataw!"

"My cousin died without son or brother, so I became

s'iam that way, not through you. But I trust you most. Except . . ."

Kwamu broke off his words. Kah-te was hurrying to the shed, and he stirred restlessly. Every line of her body aroused him.

"The Squamish *sia'm* Atsaian waits," Kah-te said, looking down to avoid the lustful look she knew would be on Kwamu's face.

"Tell him we're coming," replied Kwamu. Kah-te's indifference annoyed him, but he anticipated a conversation with Atsaian. He also welcomed interruption of his father's criticism. Turning to Paw-neset, he said, "Atsaian usually hurries upriver. Strange that he camps here. There's a reason for this visit."

At the house front the men clasped arms. Of similar age, Kwamu and Atsaian resembled each other because of their sloping heads and wide cheeks, but their markings differed. Kwamu had a small beard and had plucked his eyebrows into a fine line, whereas Atsaian was beardless with a slender moustache; for this day he had accented his face with mica. Kwamu was taller and more powerful. But Atsaian strutted with self-importance, and that suggested a larger stature.

"*Kloshe tumtum mika chako* [welcome]," said Kwamu. "We Musqueam greet our Squamish brother!"

"We thank the Musqueam for sharing the *tsukai.*"

Kwamu and Atsaian spoke in the trade jargon. The Squamish dialect and rapid mode of speaking were radically different from the Halkomelem language of the Musqueam. The jargon was necessary for communication.

"I have brought with me the Tlastlemauq people, four wives, and a daughter of age," Atsaian added after a pause.

Kwamu recognized Atsaian's reference to his wives – four to Kwamu's three – as a subtle reminder of his wealth, but he pretended not to notice. He offered clean mats to his guest and Paw-neset, and he placed one for himself. Then the three men squatted comfortably.

"A daughter of age?" Kwamu repeated.

Atsaian was quick to reply: "Ay, beautiful and high born." He cleared his throat before he said, "I offer her to you only. You have a son?"

What game is Atsaian playing? Kwamu wondered. Surely he remembers Luhk. I trust him because we don't use treachery. And Luhk does need to wed well, so I'll play his game. "I have a son," he replied, "soon to return from his *kwakwaiyiset.*"

"He'll be a hunter like you?"

"His *sulia* will decide."

Plans for his raid suddenly flashed before Kwamu! Luhk's marriage to a Squamish girl from the inlet would mean available allies. Protection, too. Boys usually wait longer, he told himself, but Luhk has skills. A wise marriage. Masking his enthusiasm, Kwamu said, "Ay, your daughter and my son." As he spoke, he looked at Paw-neset for approval, but his father was stone-faced.

Atsaian smiled. "Agreed," he said. He awaited the pertinent question, which was sure to follow when Kwamu had time to weigh the offer.

The question came. "You offer your daughter. What from me?"

Atsaian thought before he replied. To ask outright for the *Sxwaixwe* seemed presumptuous and might offend Kwamu. The trade must be delicate. "Friend of many winters," he said, "this marriage will be honour enough. I ask only one . . . er . . . favour."

"What favour?" asked Kwamu sensing the real purpose of the visit.

"The Squamish dancers want . . . want to use the

Sxwaixwe!" Atsaian held his breath because his words sounded so blunt.

Kwamu blanched and Paw-neset shifted impatiently.

"The *Sxwaixwe?* Treasure of the Stalo people?"

Atsaian pressed on. He had prepared his argument well. "The Musqueam and Squamish are almost one people. This marriage will join them by blood. Your grandson and mine, the same! Ay, we should share!"

Again Kwamu glanced at Paw-neset and received no help. Then his face lit. This is the time, he thought, to proposition Atsaian and clinch my want! "You ask a high price, *Sia'm,"* he said, "but the *Sxwaixwe* mask will be yours. Just one request."

Atsaian relaxed. He considered his point won. "Name it," he answered confidently.

Kwamu cautiously chose his words. This was a bargain between two skilled masters of the art, and it was his move.

"The Squamish fear the Euclataw and want peace," he said. "True?"

"Ay, I . . ."

Ignoring the interruption, Kwamu said, "I plan a peace to last forever."

Atsaian pretended ignorance and did not mention having discussed the plan with Te Kiapilanoq; he would grant Kwamu the satisfaction of making a sensational announcement, for he had won his own victory. "How?" he asked, acting surprised.

"With a raid on the Euclataw! A mighty raid. To stop them."

Even with prior knowledge, Atsaian shuddered at the thought of the dangerous mission. "Ah, when?"

"When chill winds blow. We'll fish and have the marriage first." Then Kwamu described the attack as he had organized it.

Nodding occasionally, Atsaian asked a few questions. "Ay," he said finally, "I'll lend Squamish warriors."

Kwamu and Atsaian stood. They raised their palms skyward and touched them together to cement their contract. The marriage, they agreed, would take place while the Squamish were still on the river; to wait would delay the raid too long.

"My son will come for the marriage after you fish at the Falls," promised Kwamu. "We'll copy the *Sxwaixwe* for you. Then after the wedding, we raid!"

Atsaian cried, "May spirits keep the Euclataw away from us!"

"And fill the river with Salmon People!"

With a final bow to Paw-neset, Atsaian disappeared through the alders as he headed for his canoe.

2

By the time his ordeal ended, Luhk had lost both sense of direction and ability to reason. One thought filtered into awareness: he had met his *sulia,* received his *syowen* [ancestral song], and could go home.

Bruised, bleeding, and near collapse, he floundered aimlessly, only to plunge farther into the forest. He had fled from the stream he was following when he came upon bear cubs and knew the she-bear was near.

His memory was hazy. The storm as he entered the woods was a blur: a rising wind, cracks of thunder, lightning, then a thud of hail and a deluge of water. In his mind, the storm blended into a supreme moment of terror, an hysteric contact with something unreal – something with shape but without shape, something with movement yet without movement. A conglomeration of animal cries and forest noises screamed into his consciousness, hypnotizing him. The bear – no, it was a cougar – crashed into the glade, and his heart hammered in his ears with such violence that his enervated body shook convulsively. He pranced uncontrollably and shouted like a mad person. He was sure that all the spirits of the sky, the sea, and the earth were there, their powers soaring about him until he sank into babbling oblivion, yet with knowledge that he would be a hunter and that the song, dance, and facial markings of that frenzy were his.

Light filtered through a patch of firs, and Luhk came upon a misty lake. Rushes lined the shore, ducks knifed through the water, and moss festooned the trees. A scent of skunk was in the air. In the open space he saw purplish outlines in the distance. "Mountains!" he cried; from them he could determine direction.

Still incoherent, Luhk eventually found the riverbank and stumbled along it until he eached Mahli. There, the last vestige of endurance faded and he sank down in exhaustion.

When Luhk wakened many hours later, the hallucinations of the forest had become a new reality. "Cougar," he called, "you're my *sulia,* my guardian spirit. Protect me! I honour you. Never will I kill or eat the cougar!"

He arose, bathed in the river, and went to the long-house. As tradition required, no one questioned him, and he did not speak of his *kwakwaiyiset* other than to inform his father that he was a hunter. His spirit would remain latent until the winter dances, when its force would compel him to perform. He wore his breechclout and a bone pin signifying the end of puberty.

For several weeks Kwamu mentioned neither the raid nor the impending marriage. Fishing was paramount. The *tsukai* run was at its peak and survival depended on the catch.

3

Residing at the river mouth was an advantage. Salmon coming from the sea were frisky; upriver, they ceased to feed; and when they neared spawning streams, they reddened and became emaciated. So instead of canoeing upriver to fish at the Falls, most Musqueam trawled or set weirs near their villages.

For days Luhk fished with the men of Mahli and shot seals, geese, and waterfowl that hovered near the fish. Kahte helped Kwamu's wives process and dry the salmon. Other women tended fires, tied nets, waded in marshes to find roots, dug clams, made dyes, and prepared spruce roots for basket-making. All the villagers went into the bogs for berries, then boiled or dried them. Summer was a time of constant labour, but it was a happy time, such a joyful part of existence that fishermen sang to their spirits and the cacophony of voices often drifted across the water far into the night.

"We have enough *tsukai,* roots, and berries," declared Kwamu one day. "Next moon, we'll go upriver for nuts and to the mountains for hunting. But now, Atsaian has returned to his camp across the river. It's time for the wedding!"

4

Kwamu told Luhk about the wedding as matter-of-factly as he would speak of the weather. To him marriage was an economic necessity, and compatibility was only a fortunate coincidence.

"My son," he began, "you will wed the daughter of Atsaian."

Luhk stood stock-still. Though he had recovered from his mystic experience and was confident about his *sulia* and his new power, he had forgotten that maturity meant being marriageable.

"My father, I . . . I'm not ready!" he gasped.

"Watch the animals. Ask the shaman. You're man enough."

"I . . . I don't mean that," Luhk stammered. "Please, may I wait?" He knew that arguing would anger his father.

"Now, there's a proper girl. Maybe not again."

"I've never seen Atsaian's daughter!"

"She's wealthy . . . enough."

I'm confused, Luhk thought. I have feeling for Kah-te, but I dare not say that. I don't have feeling for a strange girl!

When Luhk did not reply, Kwamu continued: "A wife is useful. Have sons by this one. A first wife is a worker, a helper." He wanted to clasp Luhk in his arms, for he had been a lovable child. Then he reminded himself that a parent shows love not so much with gestures as with guidance. He smiled as he walked away.

5

Luhk sought Kah-te. Since his return from the forest, leisure time had been scarce, and he had not talked with her.

Kah-te looked pleased when he told her of the marriage.

"You'll be a whole man soon," she said softly.

"I told you before . . . I plan to marry you!"

Kah-te placed a hand over Luhk's knotted fist. "Son of my master," she said, "you probably will be *sia'm.*"

"That doesn't matter!"

"Ah, it does. Forget me!"

"I don't know her!"

"Not important. If she doesn't please you, take more wives." Then she added tartly, "Or take a slave to your bed." Studying Luhk, she knew he did not detect her irony; possibly he was unaware that Kwamu used her as a mistress.

"You and I. We'll stay the same?" Luhk asked hesitantly.

"Ay, ever."

I could enjoy this boy, Kah-te thought, give him his first time with woman. It would be a good time for me, too. But he's innocent. Better for him and the young virgin to suffer together.

6

That afternoon Kwamu told Luhk to don a blanket and directed slaves to fill two canoes with food, blankets, and other marriage gifts. Kwamu and three speakers, with Luhk between them, stood on planks laid across the gunwales and chanted family wedding songs while oarsmen rowed them across the river to Atsaian's camp. As Kwamu expected, Atsaian had barred his door. Nonetheless, the speakers began talking of the importance of the two families.

Luhk sat on his haunches, listening and not caring what was said. I might care more if I could see the girl, he thought.

After each speech, Atsaian invited the visitors into his house, but he and his family remained aloof. Both families watched slaves bring in Kwamu's gifts. Kwamu and his speakers then returned to Mahli.

Ritually, Luhk wrapped in his blanket and crouched inside Atsaian's door overnight. He moved only to relieve himself outside. A fire was the sole acknowledgement of his presence; it burned to protect Tahulet, should he try to molest her! For three days and nights he sat there, miserable and hungry, the purpose being to prove that he could endure hardship.

Each day Kwamu and the speakers returned to affirm status of both families. And each day Atsaian debated whether to accept Luhk until, finally, he ordered a slave to serve Luhk a meal; this signified agreement to the marriage proposal.

On the fourth morning, Luhk sat wearily on a pile of blankets in the centre of the room. Before long, he reminded himself, the girl will come. She can be pretty or homely. I don't care, because soon I . . . we . . . can go home.

Tahulet entered the room from a curtained corner and went to the blankets where Luhk sat. She wore a tunic of finely beaten copper, decorated with her entire collection of beads and bracelets. More ornaments dangled from her ears. Following orders, she seated herself beside Luhk but held her eyes down.

Like Luhk, Tahulet was aghast when she learned that she was to marry. She had wept in dread of leaving her family to live with a husband and strangers. The shaman and her mother had dizzied her with instructions, frightening her more.

During the final speech, Luhk turned slightly to steal a look at his bride. Sensing the motion, Tahulet glanced at him. As their eyes met, both instantly turned away. Tahulet fought terror and Luhk battled the urge to escape. Talk of marriage had seemed unreal, but actual contact was devastating! As the speaker instructed the couple to uphold family traditions, both Tahulet and Luhk throbbed with unhappiness.

To simulate thunder, a man dropped a board on the roof with a boom, announcing the *Sxwaixwe* dancers.

From a partition four dancers backed out, withdrew, then repeated the movement until they emerged fully the third time. Impressively they turned until their three-dimensional *Sxwaixwe* masks were in full view.

The Squamish used simple masks, and many had never seen the *Sxwaixwe*. They were spellbound! Tahulet quivered as the dancers burst forward and towered over her.

Beneath spined, feathered crests, vividly painted faces of the raven, beaver, sawbill duck, and two-headed serpent decorated the masks. Each had extended cheeks, a bird-beak nose, a round whorl set between horns, and a pair of knobbed eyeballs bulging from ovoid sockets. Several tongues protruded from each mouth.

The dancers wore cloaks and skirts flounced with feathers. Bands circled their calves, rattles clanked on their fingers and toes, and deer-hoof ornaments clattered at their necks. They gained momentum with each twirl. Whooping and singing, they pivoted about the couple on the blankets to "wash" them. At the end, a dancer grabbed Tahulet's right hand and another took Luhk's. With deafening chants they joined hands of the bride and groom. After Kwamu had rushed forward to pay them, they passed backwards and disappeared behind the curtain.

Atsaian spoke to his people. "I promised *Sxwaixwe* dancers at my daughter's marriage. I kept my word! We can use the *Sxwaixwe* forever!" He basked in the praise of his villagers, then added, almost as an afterthought, "We thank the noble *sia'm* Kwamu!"

Kwamu bowed. He wondered how well Atsaian would keep his part of the bargain when the time came for the raid.

In the system requiring wealthy fathers to outdo each other, the ritual continued. Kwamu presented more blankets, and Atsaian tossed out another pile.

When families and guests gathered on the riverbank to watch the departure of the wedding party, Tahulet walked with her small step to the waiting canoes. Two women of rank accompanied her, and slaves carried her belongings. Numbly she seated herself in a canoe. At his father's nudging, Luhk paid the women and took a place behind her.

Atsaian drew attention to several canoes filled with food, designating them as part of his wedding gift, with the remainder to be delivered later. He added some blankets for Luhk to distribute in Mahli at the time he would invite villagers to meet his bride. After several speakers made final flattering remarks about the generosity of both fathers, boats of the wedding party moved into the stream.

Tahulet sat quietly. The late afternoon sun cast a magnificent glow on the water, but she did not enjoy it that day.

CHAPTER VI

Soon after the wedding, Atsaian and his people visited Tahulet at Mahli. They took gifts, and Atsaian's orators promised more at the birth of his first grandson.

Yearning to return to Tlastlemauq, Tahulet wistfully watched her father during the speeches. A grandson? She wondered. Her mother and the shaman had told her how a child comes, but the act they described so far had not been part of her marriage. Luhk had not come to her mat. But she said nothing; a woman, she had been told, accepts changes in her life without question.

Tahulet's bewilderment had begun after the rites when the wedding party beached at Mahli and Luhk disappeared. Slaves carried her possessions and showed her the fire pit and section of the sleeping platform that she and Luhk would use. Feeling a gentle touch on her arm, Tahulet had looked up.

Kah-te stood there. "I am your father-in-law's slave," she said. "I'll help you." She busied herself at the pit. She sparked a fire, fetched water, and clamped venison on a split stick. "Put a hot rock in this water, then . . ." She noticed that Tahulet's eyes were teary. "Your husband?" she asked, looking around.

"He . . . he doesn't speak."

"Maybe he's shy with you."

"He . . . he'll come to eat? I'm afraid."

"You both are young. Don't fear – he'll come and he'll be good to you." Kah-te spoke with more assurance than she felt, but she wanted to encourage Tahulet.

A harsh voice interrupted them. "Kah-te!"

Jumping up, Kah-te said, "One wife of my master doesn't want me here. I'll help later." She scurried across the room.

Kah-te scolded Luhk: "Talk to your wife. She's lonely."

"She's nothing to me."

"Eat with her and be pleasant. Don't anger your father."

"I didn't want to wed," Luhk argued. "My father chose her."

"She's bashful and pretty . . . Go to her," said Kah-te.

Luhk ambled to the fire pit and sat beside Tahulet. By nature kind, he had a whim of compassion. "It's hard to talk," he said. "I'll teach you some Musqueam words."

Tahulet flushed. "I'll try to learn," she replied timidly.

For the first time Luhk and Tahulet looked at each other without turning away. And in spurts of conversation during the next few weeks, they gradually became better acquainted. Night after night, however, they lay on separate mats without contact.

2

After Tahulet's family abandoned summer camp, a Mahli delegation visited Tlastlemauq. In her delight to return, Tahulet overcame some of her shyness. One afternoon after speeches she said to Luhk, "Come. I'll show you a special place." She led him to a secluded dell where a creek formed a deep pool. A carpet of moss and grasses padded the forest floor; firs and alders walled the spot. A deer bounded into a thicket at their approach.

"No current here," she said. "It's my *slalakum* place." Her face brightened with enthusiasm. Unmindful of her usual modesty, she slid out of her tunic and jumped into the water.

Luhk watched with wonder. Tahulet's animation was appealing, and he felt like a child, happy in the same kind of abandon. With a gleeful snort he flung off his breechclout and dived into the pond, splashing Tahulet and laughing with joy. Tahulet reached to him and playfully ducked his head under the water.

Spluttering, Luhk planted his feet on rocks in the pool. With a lurch he scooped Tahulet into his arms, intending to drop her in fun. But suddenly, as he gazed upon her nude body high against him, his laughter faded. Physical want overwhelmed him, a want he never had known. It was feeling neither for the wife in his arms nor for Kah-te, but an impersonal sexual craving.

Tahulet sobered, too, with awareness of Luhk's desire as he carried her from the water and put her down on the moss. The impact of his body on hers was pleasant and she trembled with sensation when he pushed her legs apart. His breath was hot on her neck. But then there was searing pain, which made her cry out, then more pain as he ignored her whimpers and kept pushing, her body pinned to the ground by his weight. She fought against him, sobbing and beating on his back with her fists. Then she felt him tense. With a final excruciating thrust he bellowed in her ear and collapsed upon her. At last, when his breathing subsided, he pulled away and lay spent beside her.

Throbbing with pain, Tahulet looked down and saw a bit of blood on one leg. With a convulsive shudder she scrambled to her feet and reeled back to the pool. The cold water eased the sting, and she wiped her tears. As she shivered in apprehension of the years ahead when her husband would make her please him this terrible way, she considered her role passively. She held no bitterness to Luhk, but she puzzled at his obvious satisfaction.

Tahulet waded from the water and put on her garment. She decided to forget the incident, at least for the present, so she could enjoy the last hours of her visit to Tlastlemauq.

Luhk lay still, relishing having performed the manly act he had heard so much about. He prickled with guilt at having caused Tahulet pain. He was not aware of being rough; as far as he knew, a woman always fought against a man. The shaman had not told him that a first experience might be difficult for a virgin bride.

Recalling words of his father, Luhk salved his concern. A wife, Kwamu had told him, was meant to prepare a man's meals, help him with chores, and satisfy his body – she expected no more. Still, he would ask Kah-te. So he rose, fastened his breechclout, and turned to Tahulet when she came from the water. "You're a real wife now," he said kindly.

Tahulet nodded and followed Luhk to the village.

3

Kwamu had gone to Tlastlemauq with more in mind than a marriage visit. His pending raid obsessed him, and he wanted to confirm Atsaian's promise to send warriors. "We'll raid now, when the swell is low on the sea," he told Atsaian. "Before we hunt."

"It's risky to tell anyone," said Atsaian. "A traitor or spy could warn the Euclataw."

"We must take that risk. Its time to alert *sia'ms*. Also some mean-men who want to go."

"Mean-men – those warriors with cruel *siwcn?*"

"Ay."

"You'll lead?" Atsaian asked. "A *sia'm* must not fight."

"I'll lead but stay in my canoe during the fight."

Kwamu informed Luhk of the raid. "At last we'll make the Euclataw suffer," he said.

"You'll let me go with you?"

"My son, I'll worry about you, selfish as that is. But

you're a man now. Ay, you may fight with the warriors."
He reached forward and squeezed Luhk's hand in a rare
gesture of caring.

Luhk disliked violence and did not realize how savage
the raid was planned to be. The permission pleased him.
"We'll free my sister?" he asked.

"If we see her. Maybe the Euclataw traded . . . or killed
her," replied Kwamu. "We'll plunder and take slaves."

Kwamu's ruthlessness and seeming disregard for his
daughter jarred Luhk. He recalled the terror of his *kwakwaiyiset* – the raid might be worse! But since the *kwakwaiyiset,* he had yearned to display his strength, and here
was an opportunity.

"Why did our sires not raid the Euclataw?" he asked.

"Their spirits did not give them power. My *sulia*
appeared in a dream and told me to raid in the last moon
of summer."

"Do the Euclataw think the Musqueam are cowards?"

"Ay, and no wonder. The Haida raids the Tsimshian,
and both raid the Euclataw. All three raid us! But now we
change that. After this raid, they'll not dare attack us again!
We'll be as terrible as they are!"

4

As unobtrusively as possible, preparations began.

Eager for combat, warriors readied their weapons.
They carved clubs with piercing knobs, honed razor-sharp
points on spears, made bone daggers for close-contact
fighting, and charred slate-tipped arrows. They fashioned
sails of woven bark matting, similar to winged devices used
by the Euclataw to increase speed. Finally, they condi-
tioned their bodies, the mean-men in particular, who had
trained for battle almost from childhood.

At Mahli, on the appointed night, warriors filled clamshells with glowing charcoal. Kwamu stepped into the lead canoe and directed his rowers to push off, paddle into a backwash, and thrust into midstream.

At Skeawatsut [Point Atkinson], other Musqueam and Squamish stroked into the current. For protection, the group travelled in close formation.

Before dawn the men rowed into a secluded cove and pulled the canoes into dense woods. They erased marks in the sand with branches and camped under cover for the day. "No motion, no fires," Kwamu ordered.

After dark on that second night, Luhk watched two mean-men knot their hair and blacken their faces, then streak in a dugout toward two men who trolled from a small boat. Daggers flashed in the moonlight. With swift, frenzied strokes the mean-men massacred the unarmed fishermen, then sank their canoe.

"Wh . . . why did they kill?" Luhk stammered.

"For luck," answered the rower behind him. "A mean-man kills before he fights. He murders the first person he meets. Two heads this time – double luck."

Luhk grimaced. He found some ways of his people distasteful but knew he was too young to challenge them.

Few of the warriors were familiar with the narrowness of the strait in northern waters, so Kwamu watched the course carefully to avoid rocks and shallows. He threaded the boats through channels, hugging shorelines as much as possible. Islands, he knew, protected the strait from swells, but crosscurrents could collapse boats in a high sea.

As the men emerged from hiding on the third night, the wind was brisk but steady. "We'll try our new sails," said Kwamu.

That night, precisely at the moment of departure, an owl screeched from an overhanging cedar. Kwamu shuddered, for the owl's cry was of reincarnated folk – an ill omen often presaging death. All heard the owl; no one commented.

Later, the moon disappeared and dark clouds scudded low. Wind built a high chop on the water, thunder rattled, and a storm broke. Frantically, oarsmen struggled to manage the sails and steer into the wind, but waves drove the canoes helter-skelter. The men shrieked for their spirits as they struggled to reach shore. Then a sheet of rain blinded them, and some boats crashed together. One engulfed canoe catapulted into a jutting rock and overturned; as the current swept the men away, their cries echoed in the howling wind until they faded and were heard no more.

When fury of the storm abated, survivors rode into shore on a back eddy. Inspecting the havoc, they nodded in understanding: the owl had spoken death.

Kwamu's band remained in hiding for several days, patching canoes, drying out supplies, and collecting every tell-tale bit of debris. They had lost eleven warriors and two canoes; Kwamu decided to attack only one longhouse.

When scouts sighted a Euclataw village, Kwamu hid his force, ordering a day of fasting before the attack. He released his command to the mean-men until after the attack.

"Black your faces," a mean-man directed. "Wear only a dagger and club. And make no sound 'til we're in the house. Then shout!"

The raiders advanced, dipping paddles without splash. The night was drizzly, almost ghostly, because clouds hid the moon and no light showed in the village. On the crest of a wave the rowers silently beached the canoes.

Half of the force approached the front entrance of a Euclataw house; others surrounded the rear door. Shrilling blood curdling war songs, the attackers burst into the house. In the faint light of hearth embers they saw men, women, and children rise screaming from their mats. With delirious chants they clubbed, slashed, and slaughtered.

Men of the longhouse had no chance to find weapons, nor could anyone escape to a stockade or refuge.

Viciousness of the onslaught shocked Luhk, specially that of the mean-men, whose actions seemed almost inhuman. Shouts of the raiders and wails of the victims sounded unearthly to him. He shuddered with horror when he saw one mean-man, then another raise a severed head and drink dripping blood! Then he felt a choking hold on his throat. Instinctively he lunged, and the dagger in his hand sank into flesh. There was a moan, the fingers loosened from his neck, and a body fell at his feet. He had killed!

"Sing so we'll know you!" a warrior bellowed in Luhk's ear, thrusting two women at him. "And take these to the boat! Now!"

Luhk dashed from the house, pulling the women behind him. Glancing back, he saw warriors light firebrands with their charcoal and toss them into the house, which blazed instantly.

The village was alert. From fortified houses, a rain of arrows and spears pounded the attackers as they raced to the water. Several warriors fell, but most reached the canoes. They threw more brands into Euclataw war canoes on the beach.

Knowing that escape was vital before the Euclataw could organize a counter-attack, the raiders shoved off rapidly. The oarsmen groaned with exertion; they hoisted sails in a favourable wind and rowed until dawn.

In command again, Kwamu thanked his spirit for Luhk's safety and chose a wooded lookout spot for hiding. As the warriors rested, their frenzy subsided; they guarded their prisoners and inspected Euclataw heads that the mean-men carried as trophies.

Luhk could not bear to look at the heads. Emotionally drained, he felt only remorse at the atrocity committed by his people. He stole looks at the captives – five women and two children – and he pitied them. But, he reminded himself, the raid was retaliation; and slave-taking had been the basis of native trade for centuries.

The Euclataw did not follow, and in four nights the canoes of the raiders reached home waters. Mean-men held the severed heads high in the air and impaled some on poles at the Mahli riverbank, leaving them there to rot. Celebration would come at the winter dances, several moons later.

CHAPTER VII

A pungent odour and a grey haze rose from peat bogs in the sloughs near Mahli, an indication that winter would come early.

Luhk participated in the autumn hunt, putting aside his misgivings about the raid and helping to bring in the winter meat supply: deer – almost as much a staple as *tsukai* – grouse, mountain goat, and bush rat, all plump and meaty after raising their young. "Don't take the otter or wolf," Kwamu had told him. "Spirits of the dead. Or the black bear – too much like man."

While she smoked meat at the hunting camp, Kah-te watched Luhk. She sensed his aversion to the raid. But his marriage is happier, she guessed. He'll tell me soon.

Frost whitened the land, and snow blanketed the mountain tops. Mahli people had harvested food and stacked firewood. They invited neighbours to *smetla* – the winter dancing activities!

Kwamu was eager for the ceremonials because Luhk would dance and because he could celebrate his raid. He pickled extra venison and stored enough provisions for a long session. Removing the partitions in his house, he welcomed his guests.

Spirit dancing was death and rebirth. On the first night the people pounded boards, beat deerhide drums, and gradually became more rhythmic until they rocked in unison. Triggered by the tempo, a man leaped from his seat when his spirit possessed him. Other dancers followed as they were caught by contagious spirit power. Heads bobbing, the people pounded harder; they hummed and moaned until they charged the room with exalted sensation and a mysterious sense of the supernatural.

Almost a hundred dancers performed. Some moved

slowly, some sweat profusely, and some sobbed. Occasionally, a dancer collapsed. When a man felt impelled to begin during another person's dance, two rhythms beat simultaneously.

On the second evening Luhk felt queasy and sensed that he was slipping from reality. Passively, he awaited his moment. Then, with no control of himself, he sighed deeply and let out a frenzied cry:

Haiiii, hai, oh, o,o,o,o!
Hai, hai, oh, o, o, o,o!
Hai, oh,hai, hai, oh, o, o, o!

Drummers crowded near Luhk, beating softly to coax his spirit into complete possession; they were careful not to startle him – that, they believed, could cause power to catch in his chest. As he grew more agitated, they increased momentum. When he uttered a few words of his song, they imitated the rhythm.

Somehow Luhk put on a cougar-tail cap and found a way to paint his face with markings from his *kwakwaiyiset*. His eyes were glassy, and he lost command of his body. Rising to his feet without willing himself to do so, he danced counterclockwise around the room; attendants circled with him to prevent his crashing into a fire. He tensed occasionally, then rushed forward again. Sounds came from his throat, and his feet moved in the pattern described in his forest vision. He was in the forest again, expecting the cougar to be upon him. He *became* the cougar, mimicking its motions, crouching low and pawing the ground. His body contorted, and his song rose to an ecstatic climax as he beat time and danced his dream *sulia* in agitated motion; he and his spirit were one. For the first time since his *kwakwaiyiset* he could reveal his spirit and feel emotional release from its terror. As the audience drummed more emphatically, he danced from fire to fire, on and on until, in an altered state of consciousness, he swooned at his father's feet.

Tahulet watched, enthralled. Kwamu and Paw-neset beamed with pride; both knew the spirit of the cougar would make Luhk an excellent hunter and provide him with supreme power.

More guests arrived to celebrate the raiders' victory. Warriors gathered while each mean-man tossed one wreath into the fire for each head he had taken, shrieking hysterically as it burst into flame. The people shouted, some in admiration, some in repulsion. At the end of the performance, Kwamu showered blankets on the fighters. "The Euclataw will not come again!" he cried.

Slaves brought in huge logs, and entertainment continued night after night. *Iagoos* repeated folklore; actors dramatized legends; and men gambled with bone dice.

2

Severe cold and an unusually heavy snow slowed departure of guests from the dances at Mahli. Shallows froze solidly. Geese and ducks huddled together in the marshes, and house dogs did not venture outside. As the guests left, they borrowed snowshoes and fur robes; smearing bear grease on their bodies, many abandoned rowing and portaged home.

As Tahulet watched the visitors leave, she said to Kah-te, "My family had a room under the house where we could keep warm."

"If you're cold, stay close to the fire. You could help weave a blanket," suggested Kah-te.

"I don't know how," sighed Tahulet. "My father-in-law's wives scold me. I didn't listen to my mother." She pointed forlornly to a pile of fleece.

"I'll show you," said Kah-te. But when Tahulet sat at the loom so that Kah-te could teach her, she burst into tears.

Kah-te patted Tahulet's abdomen. "You are with child?" she asked perceptively.

In her innocence, changes in her body had confused Tahulet, and she had not grasped their meaning. Now her tears vanished and she smiled. "Baby? My husband should like a baby," she said.

Though Luhk never gave fully of himself to Tahulet because of his feeling for Kah-te, he enjoyed Tahulet's body and her companionship as well. For Tahulet, however, emotion was more intense. After the agonizing experience in the dell, the pain of intercourse lessened until she could yield to Luhk without dread, later with genuine passion. At first, Luhk's mere presence had soothed her homesickness; soon acceptance grew into affection, then adoration, which was obvious to everyone but Luhk. She yearned for his love-making, but also for his praise.

"Maybe my husband will love me now," she said wistfully.

3

The river was silver with a moving mass of *swi'wa* [eulachons], and the sky was white with clouds of feasting gulls. Tahulet decided to save news of her pregnancy until after the three-week run of eulachon, because Luhk would be busy dip netting them and she with processing their oil.

When the run waned, the shaman thanked eulachon spirits in a ceremony. Then Tahulet amazed the family by standing to command attention. "The eulachon came first to my people," she said shyly. "Now the Squamish share with you. I . . . I know how the spirit came."

"Tell us!"

Tahulet glanced at Luhk and saw his surprise at her boldness, but she sensed his approval. "A Squamish woman had twins," she began. "Her husband bathed in the river. A stranger gave him some fish bones and told him to put them in the water." She paused as if she needed encouragement to continue.

"Finish your story!"

"He scattered the bones," Tahulet said, "and many eulachon came. Eulachon are a gift to you from the Squamish!"

As she listened to applause for her narrative, Tahulet flushed with success. Her eyes were on Luhk.

PART II

The Quest

CHAPTER VIII

Snowy peaks rose from islands far across the strait. The Squamish and Musqueam believed that a sea was beyond those islands, a sea that was home of the Salmon People. The *mamathni* men had come from that same sea.

The natives felt no need to expand the scope of their knowledge. Had the *A'lia* not made his dire prediction, they probably would have ignored more *mamathni* men who arrived in April 1792. They were English, in two ships. They had sailed north along the coast Francis Drake named New Albion and proceeded through the Strait of Juan de Fuca. The ships were under the command of Captain George Vancouver.

2

Like magnets, three lures were drawing explorers to the virgin northwest coast of North America. The first lure was land.

The second was a search for the Northwest Passage – a trade route from Europe to Asia to replace the long, hazardous rounding of South America or Africa. The other lure was the downy pelt of a small saltwater mammal: the sea otter.

Fifth-century Chinese navigators probably were first to examine the west coast of North America. One thousand years later, Spanish explorers claimed the Pacific coast as Spain's "Californias." But Drake seized the same territory for Queen Elizabeth in 1579. Loaded with silver and pieces of eight he had looted from Spanish ships, he was less eager to acquire land than to find the Northwest Passage and use it as an escape route to England!

In the same quest of a passage, the eccentric Greek who

called himself Juan de Fuca supposedly investigated the strait that later was named for him. Though many of his claims lacked authenticity, they sparked interest among other nations.

In 1725 Russia sent Vitus Bering to explore, and Russian traders followed, with orders to secure pelts worth high prices in Chinese markets – and to supply Catherine the Great with sea otter skins!

At that time, Spain claimed much of Central and South America and the entire North American west coast. The New Spain headquarters at San Blas, Mexico, considered all shores south of the Russian settlements available for conquest.

In 1774 Spain sent Juan Hernandez Perez on a coastal reconnaissance. Although currents prevented his making a landfall, he traded iron for pelts when Indians approached his ship in their canoes.

Spain also sent Lieutenant Bruno de Hezeta. Lieutenant Juan Francisco de la Bodega y Quadra accompanied him in a goleta and pushed on to Alaska.

England was unaware of the extent to which Spain and Russia had undermined Drake's claims in the Pacific. The Admiralty offered an attractive bonus for discovery of the Northwest Passage and, in 1776, transferred Captain James Cook from South Pacific exploration to the American Pacific coast.

Natives in whaling dugouts rescued Cook from fog and guided him into a bay Spaniards had named Boca de San Lorenzo de Nutka. Though repulsed when they saw "Nootkans" eat the bodies of enemies, Cook's crews called the spot Friendly Cove.

Only at the end of his exploration, after charting the Arctic coast, did Cook conclude that the Northwest Passage was nonexistent. On his return voyage to England, he anchored at the Sandwich Islands (later Hawaii), where natives murdered him.

Cook's final expedition conclusively established British sovereignty in the Pacific Northwest. When Cook's crews stopped at Macao after the murder, they discovered the Russian trade with China in sea otter pelts. Immediately, they involved Britain in the trade, after which the news spread explosively that a skin purchased for sixpence – or an iron hatchet – would bring one hundred dollars in China. Fur traders thronged to the Pacific Northwest.

To meet the demand for furs, the Indians increased their intertribal trade. But mass slaughter erupted as traders paid natives to club sea otters by the thousand, and the Indians lost an animal kinship as old as their existence.

The ambitious Captain John Meares arrived at Nootka in 1778 with artisans and Chinese labourers. Purchasing land for a few sheets of copper, he built a fortified house and cemented friendships with the powerful leaders Wickaninnish and Maquinna.

Explorers and early traders on the Pacific coast bartered without language and had little reason to converse with the natives. Meares, however, was an exception; he became fluent in the trade jargon and filled journals with notations valuable to historians.

Among other explorers were the Americans, who sailed for adventure and profit. Two of the most notable Americans were Captain Robert Gray in the *Columbia* and John Kendrick, the hard drinking captain of the *Lady Washington*.

As a whole, the explorers had a profound effect on native culture. To the Indian *Whiteman* had arrived!

CHAPTER IX

In England, far from the fur trading in North America, Matthew Chamberlain Stewart signed as an able-bodied seaman on a Royal Navy barque. Matt, as his family called him, lived in the port of Falmouth, where a tale of the high seas was as commonplace to a child as a fairy fable, and where the weather condition was on every tongue.

When he was a boy, Matt often meandered along cobbled streets to the waterfront. Beauty to him was a graceful full-rigged trading ship sailing before the wind.

As Matt grew older, his yen for sailing became an obsession. He liked to hurry to the wharves after classes to mingle with fishermen and merchant seamen. He listened to their yarns and boarded ships when he could, staying until dusk, when he would speed home to avoid punishment. He savoured the smell of fish and swarthy men; and he absorbed the infectious spirit of the sea. When the exciting northwest American coast filtered into conversation, it spawned in Matt a desire to sail to that part of the world.

Matt's well-to-do family had distinguished itself for several generations as business magnates. They considered his fascination for the sea as childish and tried to encourage him in more genteel pursuits.

"Put aside this folly, at least until you're older," Matt's parents urged. The Royal Navy, to their mind, was a corrupt place for men without other means of livelihood. At the same time, they recognized the career of a naval officer as respectable. Eventually, they consented to Matt's signing as an apprentice and used their influence in his being accepted at the age of thirteen. He would serve at least two years before qualifying as a midshipman and six before he could apply for a commission.

To Matt, memory of inching along a bobbing gangplank to board his ship was of hubbub: noisy sea birds, yellow-toothed sailors bawling blasphemously, merchants hawking wares, and skimpily clad women who were aboard until sailing time.

Unused to the feel of his wide-legged, duck trousers, Matt perspired with nervousness and lugged his sea chest down the companionways to a deck below the water line where ordinary seamen bunked. He took each rung gingerly, slightly nauseated by a putrid stench of urine, mildew, and stale air rising from below. Though glamour of his anticipated experience dimmed somewhat, he happily stowed his chest beside a berth.

Matt tried to ignore the contortions of a seaman and a gaudy woman until their hammock overturned and threw the half-naked pair to the planks. He smiled at two tattooed, barefooted sailors who watched him stonily. He guessed that neither had bathed for many days, and he controlled a shudder of repulsion. A voice came from the ladder: "Ahoy! Seaman Stewart!"

Startled, Matt looked into the hatch at the man above him. "Aye, sir! I'm Stewart!"

"Then hoist up your gear and come above, lad. You bunk up here in the gun room! Deck mate should've told you!" Matt was surprised by jeers of the men beside him.

"Well, blimey, if it ain't another dandy," said one with a Cockney accent, his lip curling.

"Too fancy for the likes of us, is it?"

"I . . . I don't understand," stammered Matt.

"You will, pretty boy!"

"Likely you'll be wantin' foot ropes on the rigging!"

They turned away with derisive smirks, not so much at Matt as at the system itself, in which prestige and rank often counted more than ability in gaining preferential treatment.

Matt did not reply as he shoved his sea chest up the ladder.

"I'm Perkins, the gunner," said the man who summoned him. He was in his thirties, his body toughened by exposure to salt air. He was not much cleaner than the men below, but he was kind and civil. "You'll be an officer one day, lad, so you'll do as a young gentleman." With a wink he added, "Under my nose."

Matt and other officer candidates fared better than average seamen. With a schoolmaster they studied astronomy, geography, and navigation; they learned to rig and manage sails, read chronometers, and take sightings from the stars.

Matt saw men hate and he saw men love. He saw them in cowardice and gallantry, in shame and honour. He saw men cheat, and he saw them give lives for friends. A port, he learned, meant going ashore to consort with a woman, and he discovered that some men found pleasure with one another.

And Matt saw men die. He watched some become listless from scurvy, then progressively worse until teeth fell from rotting gums, skin ulcerated, and death came as a merciful release. He saw others die from consumption, dysentery, knife wounds, and from brutal lashes of cat-o'-nine-tails. He became a man.

At sixteen, as a midshipman, Matt stood watches, chalked reports, and worked sails. All crew members shared the same scurvy-prone diet, but with cheques from his father he secured additional food and hired a hammock man to lash lice from his bedding.

He grew tall and vigorous. His eyes were a luminous green, and the sun lightened his auburn-red hair. He was popular with officers and peers. But in his fifth year as midshipman, wind hurled him to the deck when he was shortening sail. With fractures of both legs, he spent the remainder of the voyage in sick bay. When the ship put in at Southampton, he went home to recover.

During his convalescence, Matt read *A Voyage to the Pacific Ocean,* the official, three-volume account of Captain James Cook's expedition. Longing for the sea, he again resolved to see North America. "One more year for a commission," he reminded his family when they urged him to enroll at Oxford.

The Admiralty announced a voyage by Captain Henry Roberts, who had sailed with Cook: a voyage to continue Cook's explorations and, more importantly, to expand Great Britain's Pacific trade. Matt's legs had healed; he did not hesitate.

2

Alarmed by British trade at Nootka, by Russian advances, and by American intervention, Spain in 1789 dispatched Don Esteban Jose Martinez and Gonzalo Lopez de Haro to oust foreign traders and to claim the coast south of Alaska. Ignoring the Union Jack waving over the Meares outpost at Nootka, Martinez took possession of the entire area for Spain. He captured two British trading ships, intimidated the Americans, destroyed all fortifications, and sailed to Mexico with British prisoners.

Parliament, already incensed by other Spanish offenses, immediately appropriated funds for war and alerted its allies, Prussia and Holland. It cancelled the Roberts voyage.

Rather than face the largest British fleet ever mobilized, Spain capitulated and restored British claims in 1790 at the Nootka Convention in Madrid. The North American Pacific coast would be Spanish and Catholic only as far north as San Francisco.

Guaranteed trade freedom, the Admiralty revived its Pacific expedition plan. This time the command went to Lieutenant George Vancouver.

Promoted to Master and Commander, Vancouver received his orders: to gain formal restitution of Nootkan property, to consolidate British military strength in the Pacific, to survey inlets and rivers from latitude 30 degrees to 60 degrees north, and to conduct a final search for the fabled passage through North America.

Vancouver would command a three-masted, square-rigged sloop of war of 340 tons bearing the name of Cook's barque, the *Discovery;* the ship would carry a crew of one hundred. His consort tender would be the *Chatham,* an armed, two-masted, 135 ton brig with forty-five men under Lieutenant and Commander William Robert Broughton.

With flags flying, the *Discovery* worked down the Thames with the tide from the Deptford shipyards to Long Reach, where she took on additional ordnance and equipment. After stops at Spithead, Plymouth, and Guernsey, she sailed through the English Channel to Falmouth. There, at the jetty, she met the *Chatham,* manned and brimming with supplies. And there Midshipman Matt Stewart boarded the *Discovery.*

Both ships skimmed out of the harbour, clearing break-waters at dawn on April 1, 1791. Vancouver chose Cook's route around the Cape of Good Hope and across the Indian Ocean. From Australia he planned a northeasterly course to North America.

CHAPTER X

"Land ho!" Matt ran to the bow. The American continent, at last! As the *Discovery* and the *Chatham* glided landward, late afternoon sun glistened on white beaches, and waves broke in bubbly crescents. He stared at the land he had yearned to see. To him, the past year was but a prelude to this moment, to reaching North America! He thought of his months on the *Discovery.*

He recollected the first assembly, called as soon as the ships were at sea, sails billowing. "All hands, ahoy! Turn out, aft!" the boatswain cried. A Marine corps stood rigidly at attention, scarlet uniforms blazing in the sun, and Vancouver paced back and forth.

Matt studied the captain, resplendent in a gilt-trimmed, blue uniform with knee breeches, a long-tailed waistcoat, and a brass-buttoned vest. George Vancouver, a bachelor, was thirty-four years of age, but his thin lips, jowled face, and powdered queue suggested age. He rarely smiled, and his eyes held no sparkle.

Carrying himself erectly, Vancouver had an air of dignified refinement. He faced his men, holding his bicorn hat against his breast. "I'll run a tight ship," he began sternly. "I've hand chosen most of you, so I expect dedication. I'll punish laziness and disobedience. There will be no scurvy – we use spruce beer, sauerkraut, and fresh meat – you see animals in the deck pen yonder. And I expect galleys free of vermin, decks swabbed and fumigated daily. Also daily – every man to bathe in salt water."

Vancouver paused, then introduced the officers beside him: "My Master, Mr. Joseph Whidbey, and Lieutenants Mudge, Puget, and Baker." With a frown, he motioned to another man. "And this is Mr. Menzies," he said, "Royal Navy surgeon, botanist on this voyage for the Royal

Gardens." Pointing to the *Chatham,* he added, "On the tender there, Mr. Broughton has Mr. Johnstone as master and navigator. Now, all hands to stations! One hour before supper will be leisure time."

Remembering, Matt thought of winds humming in taut rigging, of the sea rolling white before the bow at first light, and of quiet nights when the stars were so brilliant they seemed near enough to touch. He thought, too, of hail and sleet at Cape Horn. And of being becalmed while skirting the African coast; sails had flopped limply and the men had groaned with boredom until a sudden tempest pitched the ships into mountainous wave troughs that seemed headed to the bottom of the sea.

Another storm had battered the ships near New Zealand while most of the crew slept. As the watch studied ominous barometric readings, wind and sheets of rain burst all at once. Lightning catapulted across the sky, the ship creaked, and the towering sea washed over the quarterdeck. The *Discovery,* hit broadside, heeled and rolled. Men crashed from their hammocks, and gear ran loose. Vancouver charged on deck with a cape over his nightshirt; "Turn all hands! Strike the topgallants! Reef the topsail!" he bellowed. Crewmen fought to batten hatches and secure stays, but spray stung their faces and they had to cling to the rails for their lives. Fuming, Vancouver grabbed the helm, put the tiller hard over, and turned the ship into swells to ride out the storm.

"Ye gods, what a stench!" the men complained after each storm, when pumps and smudge pots did not control the odour of bilge sloshing in the waterlogged hold.

Monotony, a penetrating chill, and the gloom of candles burning blue wore on the crews. Limited space exaggerated confinement, and the men became cranky.

Officers and seamen observed Vancouver's depression.

His rages, unusual spurts of energy, and occasional irrationality had been apparent from the first week of the voyage, but they became more frequent. His right eye seemed to puff when he was angry.

2

Matt reminisced about days in Australia and Tahiti. Tahiti! Otaheite! After the storms, the name itself had been a panacea for suffering. As the ships neared land, the sea calmed and the men gazed longingly on waterfalls and serene lagoons. A fragrant land breeze tantalized them and prompted lively talk of women generous with favours.

"The Tahitians are rascals, you know," warned Puget.

"And they'll steal before your eyes," commented Mudge.

"Nothing, absolutely nothing will keep me from one of those beauties," argued McKenzie, a midshipman.

Puget chuckled, then added, "The captain's afraid of more than theft, actually. Seamen before us have brought diseases to the natives, and he wants us to avoid contamination."

The Tahitians swarmed about the ships in long outriggers, displaying their wares. *"Taio,"* [friend], they cried. Amber-skinned maidens in grass skirts raised their arms invitingly.

The sailors whistled and cheered.

At anchor, Vancouver stunned both crews. "No shore leave!" he ordered. "I want no disease – or theft."

"Bide your time, m'hearties," said a mate. "The captain'll try to show off – that'll be our night."

As the seaman guessed, Vancouver entertained with fireworks, and natives clambered over the gunwales. "Noble savages they are," he muttered in disgust at the women slinking on his ships.

The officers ridiculed Matt because he refused to take a woman to his berth.

Matt tried to explain. "I don't know why exactly. I bedded once on another ship and I felt . . . disgusted with myself."

3

Vancouver's moods became incidents in themselves. He was overly irate when the storeship *Daedalus* did not rendezvous on schedule. Though he needed the *Chatham* to carry supplies and assist in attack, he fumed that she was exasperatingly slow.

"A martinet," Matt heard officers call Vancouver when they were grumbling at his rigidity. But Matt was fond of the captain. He remembered a chat with his bunkmates as they sampled a new supply of spruce beer.

"A man could live on this stuff if it didn't pucker the mouth," commented Matt, wiping his lips.

"'Tis bitter but beats bein' down with scurvy."

"Well, like it or not, if the captain said drink, we'd drink," commented McKenzie. "Or take the lashes!"

Matt looked up. "You're thinking of the two dozen Pitt had today." He referred to Thomas Pitt, a fellow midshipman whom they disliked.

"Hot temper the lad has. He deserved it."

"The captain's strict, I'll grant you," said Matt, "but he says there'll be no mutiny on a tight ship."

"Mutiny might be what we need! But Pitt – shouldn't he behave better? He's nobility, isn't he?" McKenzie queried.

"That's right," replied Matt. "He's the Honourable Thomas Pitt. From Cornwall, like me. Maybe he needs discipline – he's always quarrelsome." He paused, then said, "Y'know, the captain has to enforce rules to protect us. I feel sorry for him."

"Sorry! Whatever for?"

"He's by himself. Without friends."

"Well, he has the officers. They're close in age."

Perhaps awareness of Matt's concern caused Vancouver to prefer him to the other midshipmen and to treat him like a son. An unspoken bond of trust and understanding developed between the two. Vancouver also realized that Matt had served six years as midshipman and could take commission examinations if he were in England. He regarded him accordingly – as almost an officer, worthy of choice assignments. Though Matt's friends teased about his being the favourite, they acknowledged his rank, and none but Pitt felt undue jealousy.

CHAPTER XI

Moving north of New Albion, Vancouver began an intricate survey. Often he lowered his boats to examine waters too shallow for the ships to navigate. Charting every cove and inlet, he searched relentlessly for the Northwest Passage.

The afternoon of April 28th was stormy, the sea running high, the barometer falling, and the wind screaming. Squalls whipped over the decks that night, and the next day was rainy.

Mist obliterated a cleft in coastal mountains, which would have suggested the presence of a river. Vancouver noticed silt flowing into the sea but decided to investigate it later, thus missing the mouth of the Columbia River.

"Sail ho! Heave to!"

A ship approached, hoisting American colours on its mainmast. It fired a volley of welcoming guns. "Halloa!"

"What ship is that?" called Vancouver, as he drew up astern, returned the gunfire salute, and raised his own flag.

"The *Columbia!* Captain Robert Gray in command!"

Vancouver dizzied with pleasure in unexpectedly meeting the reputedly reckless Gray. Securing permission, he sent Puget and Menzies aboard to question Gray about his earlier voyages. Then he spread a chart before the midshipmen. "See here," he said, "I've been theorizing about this body of land behind Nootka. I think it's a freestanding island and I want to be first to circumnavigate it. Gray supposedly entered an inland sea north of Nootka. What luck for him to verify that!"

"Captain Gray laughed about that," Puget reported, "because he went only a few miles into the Strait of Juan de Fuca. The natives told him of a northern passage, he said, but he ignored the information." Hesitantly, he added, "Gray plans to stop at the place we noticed silt. He said he stood off breakers there for days and couldn't get through the surf. But he's sure there's a river there – the Spaniard Hezeta mentioned it, too – and he intends to enter this time and claim it for America."

"He had another reason to hurry south," said Menzies. "Devilish business it was. He wanted to build a sloop, so he put up some cabins with cannons near Nootka and called them Fort Defiance. Well, he had a Sandwich Island native with him, and Wickaninnish bribed the man to wet the cannon priming. Gray said the Nootkans probably planned to murder his whole crew, but he escaped and had his revenge by destroying an Indian village."

The officers made sarcastic remarks about American ways, and Vancouver silenced them by ordering full sail. He smarted at his humiliating blunder in not taking the alleged river for England.

With the tide in their favour, the ships left the outer waters, rounded a headland Cook had named Cape Flattery, and entered the Strait of Juan de Fuca. Was it possible, some of the crew mused, for the ships to be entering the long-sought Northwest Passage? They chattered with supposition.

Still unaware that Barkley, Eliza, Martinez, and Narvaez had preceded him, Vancouver dismissed the de Fuca and Gray voyages as being too brief. Cook denied a passage but missed this entrance, he told himself. He preferred discovery, but I like charting. Yet perhaps *I* can be the discoverer here!

Intrigued, Matt watched singing natives in canoes encircle the ships, calling out in language a few sailors recognized as the trade jargon. The Indians had streaked their faces, oiled their noticeably grimy bodies, and pleated their hair with strands of seaweed. Some picked lice from their bodies and chomped them between their teeth. The men wore ornaments in their ears and cloaks over their shoulders, leaving most of their bodies naked. The women were more modest, in fringes hanging from waistbands.

2

Vancouver let some Indians board to barter fish for beads and blue cloth, but the natives pointed to metal items: knives, kettles, iron pots, and brass uniform buttons – even offering two children for a sheet of copper! These natives were so filthy that Vancouver ordered them off his ships. He chose a sheltered harbour, which he named New Dungeness.

Vancouver attached names of royalty, friends, and his officers to most of the landmarks he mapped. When Baker called attention to a prominent snow-capped peak, Vancouver dubbed it Mount Baker. Little did he know that Indians associated that volcanic mountain with the great-flood story of their origin or that the Spanish had named it La Montana del Carmelo.

In a harbour he called Port Discovery, Vancouver halted the expedition for two weeks to replenish supplies and overhaul both ships. When smiling Indians offered wares and their women, he advised against bringing women aboard but did not forbid it.

"Egad, they're dirty!" said McKenzie.

"Begging your pardon, sir, you can scour 'er first, y'know!" a seaman remarked.

As Matt watched, his friends brought tubs on deck and filled them with water. They unclothed the women, plunged them into the bath, and soaped their bodies. Then they hastened below, each with a woman in tow. What an indelicate procedure, Matt thought, to be so arousing! Again, he refused to have a woman.

Later, the crews were happy to move into waters of the Coast Salish Indians, where dress and cleanliness improved.

3

"Stock the boats well," Vancouver ordered after leaving Port Discovery. "We'll do precise mapping here." He assigned men to the *Discovery's* launch and yawl, and to the *Chatham's* cutter. At least one boat landed at each outstanding point, where the officers recorded soundings and compass bearings. Welcome was uncertain until natives offered fish, women, and berries; and in one deserted spot the men found human heads impaled on sticks.

Vancouver named a large arm of the strait Puget Sound for his second lieutenant. He examined the present sites of Tacoma, Everett, Seattle, and Bremerton; he named Admiralty Inlet, Mount Ranier, Hood Canal, and Whidbey Island; and he titled all land north of New Albion as New Georgia. On June 4th, to honour His Majesty King George III on his birthday, he issued a double ration of grog and excused all work except hauling in the seines. Though Eliza had named the strait one year before, Vancouver took possession for Britain, calling it the "Gulph" of Georgia.

4

"Boatswain! Out boats!" The ships had anchored in a cove that Vancouver labelled Birch Bay because Menzies noticed some black birch trees. "We'll explore again," he said. "Mr. Puget and I will head north." He issued work orders for crew remaining with the ships, then barked,

"Mind yourselves, for Mr. Broughton will inform me of shirkers."

Puget manned the launch, and Matt tended sails on the yawl, occasionally taking the tiller. At camp one evening Vancouver departed from his customary reserve. "So many natives are scarred or minus an eye from pox," he said. "God knows Cook didn't bring pox, but I'm convinced white presence hasn't helped natives."

"Hmmm, an unusual thought," said Menzies, whom the captain had come to trust. "I'd like to hear you discuss this."

"So would I, sir," said Matt.

Vancouver said no more, but many years later Matt was to recall the conversation.

5

At the 49th parallel Vancouver named Point Roberts for the original leader of the expedition. Continuing north, he held both boats offshore because of sand bars at the mouth of the Fraser River, which Narvaez had discovered for Spain in 1791. *"I suspect a river at flood stage with submerged islands,"* he recorded in his journal, but he mapped the area as bays and inlets.

Weary crews hoisted sails after midnight and crossed the channel to a rocky island where sea lions forced them to sleep in the boats. Returning to the mainland on June 13th, Vancouver gave the name Point Grey to Ulksn. Again he looked at the swampy delta, noted that it was navigable only by canoe, and saw the village of Mahli. He explored English Bay. Then, with a breeze, he led the boats through the Narrows into the inlet, which he named Burrard's Channel in recognition of a friend. As the day was showery, he hoped to seek shelter early. "Furl sails," he ordered, "and keep offshore until we find a place to camp."

A tumultuous welcome by Musqueam and Squamish in the inlet surprised the crews! Eager to trade for whiteman's riches, each Indian group touted its village as a landing spot. An ornate canoe bore Te Kiapilanoq. Paddlers knelt, drummers beat rhythm, and dancers cavorted on planks laid across the bows. Natives tossed the down of waterfowl into the air – their way of warding off disaster – but as the clouds of feathers fell softly over the boats, the crews interpreted them as a token of friendship.

Sighing, Vancouver said to the rowers, "Rest your oars. We can't escape trading."

Kwamu had brought Luhk to Tlastlemauq – and Tahulet, waddling uncomfortably in her last month of pregnancy. When scouts had reported Vancouver's approach, Kwamu told Luhk to pack a canoe with fish and blankets. For himself he chose a small dugout, and he commanded Kah-te to put on a hooded cloak and get in his boat.

As soon as possible, Vancouver halted the trading and resumed his search for a camp site – one, he hoped, of privacy from overly friendly natives. He ordered short sail.

At dusk the boats were about twelve miles within the Narrows, near the head of the inlet. Only three canoes followed.

Despairing of cliffs and stony beaches, Vancouver ordered his crews to pull in at a rocky shore, secure the boats to trees with hawsers, and disembark for the night. The rain stopped.

6

Kwamu paddled one of the canoes that followed. In one end of his dugout, Kah-te crouched in fright, wondering if he brought her to trade to a whiteman for copper. She wished that Luhk had stayed in the procession; he had returned to Tlastlemauq when the trading ended.

Kwamu laughed with the other Indians when the sailors grappled with a seine and pulled it in empty. He watched the other Indians land, offer fish, and gesture that they would bring more in the morning. He sat quietly in his boat when they became bolder and pointed to muskets stacked on the beach.

Fretful, Vancouver had shed his earlier compassion for the Indians. "They're a bloody nuisance," he grumbled. "I'll show some grape so they'll leave." Loading several muskets, he fired one into the woods, and the Indians shied away.

Kwamu had no fear. He leaped from his boat, grabbed another gun that Vancouver had loaded, and fired it. The kick and the blast so close to his ear stunned him, but he smiled proudly.

When Vancouver signalled that the play was over, the other canoes pulled off, but Kwamu remained where he stood on the beach. I must have that magic stick, he decided. It makes a bigger noise than Atsaian's! "Kah-te," he called, "cover your face and wrap yourself!" Pulling her behind him, he approached seamen who were setting up tents. He pointed to the musket he had fired and thrust Kah-te forward as exchange, making obscene motions to indicate that she was good for a night of pleasure. He had concealed her body because he thought her natural appearance would be repulsive.

The men glanced only fleetingly at the hooded girl and assumed that she resembled other Musqueam and Squamish women.

"No, no, we don't want her," said Johnstone, turning away.

Vancouver was busy at the far side of the clearing. Noting this, a few midshipmen whispered together. "One musket he wants, and we can have his woman for the whole night!"

"Well, it's not worth it to me to scrub one of them again!" an officer replied. "Besides, we agreed those crazy deformed heads are sickening!"

The midshipmen conferred in an undertone.

"Sir," said McKenzie to Puget, "we suggest giving this woman to Stewart! He hasn't had a turn for months!"

Puget grinned. "Capital idea," he said.

"I'd rather not," interrupted Matt.

Knowing he risked severe punishment by the captain, McKenzie furtively slipped the musket to Kwamu and whisked Kah-te to Matt.

"She's yours now, man," he told Matt. "Be off down the beach with her! We'll check, so be sure you perform!"

Matt decided to humour his friends, intending to go with the woman but to ignore her. With a shrug he picked up his blanket and followed Kah-te around a bend of the shore.

Kah-te did not consider disobeying Kwamu; she rejoiced that he was not trading her permanently. She found a native trail through the brush to a small beach away from the camp, its pristine stillness pierced only by a waterfall cascading from a cliff and spraying on the rocks below. She stopped, turned to Matt, and removed the cloak from her body.

Matt gasped at Kah-te's beauty, so unlike what he had expected. She wore no paint; her head was natural with short, glossy black hair; and her body was clean, tanned, gleaming with health, and completely voluptuous. His gaze fell to her full, high breasts as she casually unfastened her short apron and stood naked before him.

Kah-te did what was expected of her. But as she watched the tall man with light skin and head plain like hers, his shyness touched her and she found him attractive. He did not shove her to the ground, and he seemed embarrassed. She felt compassion and a want she never had known – the desire for this man to hold and caress her while she would make him happy. She reached up and stroked his cheek. Then her fingers went to his tie; she loosened it and slid the shirt off his arms.

Kah-te was desirable. Matt forgot his aversion to native women. When she groped at his belt, he unfastened the buckle and let his sea breeches fall to the ground.

Raising one hand, Kah-te ran to the edge of the brush, plucked two leaves from a shrub, and rubbed one against Matt's arm to show the soapy feel of it. She grasped his hand and led him to the waterfall. Wetting one leaf, she began to gently wash Matt – his arms, his face and chest, his legs – and she noticed how eager he was for her as she handed him the other leaf.

Matt wet the leaf and stroked Kah-te's arms with it. Joyfully, both stepped under the icy waterfall. Matt washed Kah-te's hair and face and then, hesitantly, his hands slid down her body. In unison of desire, they moved together.

Tense and shivering, they came out of the water. Quickly Matt spread his blanket in a sandy space between two rocks and they rolled in it to dry and warm themselves. Matt's lips met Kah-te's, something new and pleasurable to her, and then tenderly Matt made love.

Thrilling to Matt's touch and learning from him, Kah-te fondled him. He was gentle, then in ecstasy thrust himself fully, again and again. Climax came to both in the same exultant moment, glorious and exhausting.

As Matt stilled, his brain throbbed. I'll never forget this woman who has satisfied my wildest fantasy, this woman I can't talk to. My family expects me to marry and have sons to carry on the name. A prim wife will never make love like this! Had I found this woman under different circumstances, I could have shared my life with her! I can't take her with me. But I can return!

Darkness had come. A moon partially lit the beach, and the sky was bright with stars. Matt and Kah-te lay quietly, huddled in the blanket. At first, an aura of understanding made language unnecessary. Then each felt a compulsion to speak of their relationship, and they struggled for communication because Matt knew only a few words of the jargon.

Kah-te pulled an arm free of the blanket, sat up, and with a piece of driftwood drew two stick figures in the sand, gesturing that one was he, the other she. Then she placed a hand on her abdomen and showed it getting larger with rounding motions. She drew a third smaller figure and looked at Matt, smiling. *"Tenas* [baby]," she said.

Matt understood and nodded. "You will have a baby. Mine." He could not ask how she was so sure.

Kah-te had no question; she knew instinctively.

They continued the sand drawings. Matt sketched the ships, showing them going across the sea. Then he drew a single figure, beckoning to himself, on a ship sailing back to her.

"Mika killapie [you return]," Kah-te said.

They laughed, hugged, and then Matt sobered. He kissed Kah-te long and passionately, and they had intercourse again. Afterward, they dozed, holding each other tightly. Time was at a standstill.

A whistle shrilled through the woodland and across the water. Matt leaped up in alarm. It was still dark, but the boats must be ready to leave!

The moon had disappeared and a fresh breeze had

risen, chilling the air and whipping waves onto the shore. Hastily, Matt dressed and snatched the blanket, while Kah-te fastened her skirt about her waist and gathered the cloak under her arm.

Matt clung to Kah-te in a last embrace, and his head spun with the momentary desire to hide and stay there forever. But the whistle pierced the air again! Quickly they drew apart and ran along the path to the boats.

As Matt and Kah-te emerged from the woods, some of the men saw them and began to snicker. Then, in the light of their fading fire, they saw Kah-te for the first time without the cloak, and their mirth faded.

"Blimey, she's a beauty!"

"And to think some of us had to sleep in the boats after the tide came in and swamped us!"

"Aye, a ghastly night – and see what Stewart had!"

Matt smiled, hugging Kah-te to him. "I thank you!" he said.

Then Vancouver caught sight of Matt. "So, Mr. Stewart," he said flatly, "you're back. All hands, prepare to shove off! Put out the fires and load the gear!"

Matt pressed Kah-te to him and, with motions he hoped she understood, he repeated his promise to return. On impulse he unfastened from his belt a small gold horseshoe that he wore for luck, and placed it in her palm.

"To remember me," he said. He showed her his initials engraved on the back of the charm. Then he hurried off to the yawl.

A bleak dawn was breaking, with clouds racing against the mountains, and the wind blew colder. Kah-te shivered and put on her cloak. She clutched the charm and watched until the boats were out of sight. Though she grieved because her lover was gone, she felt joy – an emotional awakening she knew would stay with her. Now, she consoled herself, when Kwamu has me, I'll pretend he's my *tel-cha* [stranger from afar] with hair like fireweed.

Kwamu appeared from a cove where he had spent the night. He stroked his new musket and made no comment when he pulled ashore and Kah-te climbed into the boat.

He's too busy with his gun to think about me, Kah-te noted with relief.

7

As he left the inlet he had named Burrard's Channel, which later was called Burrard Inlet, Vancouver recorded an observation. He certainly had no premonition that he was describing the site of the great city that would bear his name – Vancouver:

The portside shore is of a moderate height, though rocky, well covered with trees of large growth, especially of the pine tribe.

Deciding to seek shelter from the rising wind, he turned into a sound, naming it for Earl Howe, First Lord of the Admiralty. A squall bore down, and the men anchored in a cove. When the weather improved, the two boats worked north to another finger of the strait, which Vancouver named Jervis Inlet. Then they headed back to Birch Bay.

Still mesmerized by Kah-te's warmth, Matt let his emotions race. He did not know Kah-te's name, yet he wanted to abandon ship to remain with her. He vowed that he would return to her.

CHAPTER XII

At Birch Bay Broughton was in command during Vancouver's absence.

"Ship ahoy!" called the watch shortly before dawn of June 13th. Two schooners were in the strait, and when Broughton gave chase in the *Chatham,* they ran up Spanish flags.

Missing this will devastate the captain, Broughton told himself. Boarding one of the ships, the *Sutil,* he saluted the commander, Don Dionisio Alcala Galiano. With the sister ship, piloted by Don Cayetano Valdes, Galiano was surveying.

"On behalf of Captain George Vancouver I pledge any help we can give our Spanish friends," said Broughton formally, remembering that the Admiralty expected co-operation.

"Gracias," replied Galiano, who understood English and spoke with a heavy accent. He showed his maps.

After Galiano and Valdes departed, they anchored at the mouth of the Fraser and confirmed the Narvaez discovery of a wide-mouthed river. Kwamu spotted them there and, eager to bargain for another musket, shoved Kah-te into his dugout.

Kah-te knelt expectantly, hoping she would see her lover again. But soon she realized that these ships were not the boats she had seen in the inlet and that the men on deck were different.

Kwamu shook his head when the Spaniards offered knives and abalone shells for his salmon and arrows. Pointing to muskets and some iron grillwork on the ship, he thrust Kah-te forward, but the Spaniards withdrew.

2

Nearing Birch Bay in his yawl, Vancouver gasped when he rounded a promontory and came upon the Spanish ships. He grabbed his glass and shook with emotion. "Mr. Puget, get permission to board and go with me. You, too, Mr. Stewart. What in blazes are the Spanish doing here?" he raged.

With effusive hospitality, Galiano showed charts proving he had been at that point one year earlier. Vancouver responded with charm, but he struggled to control his astonishment when the Spaniards described additional ventures into inland waters. Masking his pride and humiliation, Vancouver invited Galiano and his two ships to travel with the *Discovery* and the *Chatham.*

"Señor," replied Galiano, "perhaps you should turn back to Nootka Sound. I bear a message from Don Juan Francisco de la Bodega y Quadra!"

"Quadra? He's at Nootka?"

"He's waiting for you there with three frigates and a brig!"

"And was a storeship from England also there for me?"

"I saw none."

Hmm, thought Vancouver. If the *Daedalus* is not there with my orders, I can't negotiate with the Spanish or accept property for Britain. The meeting with Quadra can wait! Smiling, Vancouver accepted Galiano's offer to examine the part of Burrard Inlet that he had missed, then share findings.

When he was back on the yawl, Vancouver shed his affability. "I'm mortified," he stormed to Puget. "The Spaniards have explored every cove!" Without waiting for a reply, he continued: "I'm piecing together puzzling things like the iron-tipped spears and European axes we've found and how seeing a sailing ship doesn't surprise most natives."

"What do you conclude?" asked Puget.

"That the Viceroy of Mexico has blatantly ignored provisions of the Madrid Nootka Convention!" Vancouver shouted. Veins stood out on his temples. "Eliza is back at Nootka with a flotilla! By no means has Spain stopped fighting for territory – or trying to find the Northwest Passage!"

Subduing his vexation, Vancouver told his crew to move on. Flood tides still obscured the river delta, but he stopped long enough to trade for some fresh sturgeon.

3

Unaware that Kah-te lived at a river village, Matt had no idea he was near her that day. But she, seeing the yawl, began to run to it. Suddenly, Kwamu stepped ahead of her in the path.

Kah-te never dared resist her master, but this time she struggled desperately to free herself from his grip. "Let me go!" she pleaded.

Ruthlessly, Kwamu pushed her to the ground, slapped her across her face, and raped her. When it was over and she staggered to the riverbank, the yawl was gone.

4

Winds were so contrary that the rowers camped overnight at Point Roberts. Exhausted when they reached Birch Bay, they yanked themselves to the deck on ropes and collapsed.

When the Vancouver ships met Galiano, he reported finding only a narrow river at the end of the inlet – no passage.

Then the four ships set sail, and Vancouver quickly became disillusioned. His ships were faster, and his thoroughness clashed with more casual methods of the Spanish. He found further evidence that explorers and merchants had preceded him, and the terrain depressed him so much that he named one inlet Desolation Sound, describing it in his journal:

Our residence here was truly forlorn; an awful silence pervaded the gloomy forests, whilst animated nature seemed to have deserted the neighbouring country . . . Nor was the sea more favourable to our wants. The steep rocky shores prevented use of the seine, and not a fish at the bottom could be tempted to take the hook.

Though the quest for the Northwest Passage discouraged him, Vancouver still hoped to prove the existence of an island by circumnavigating it. He had his proof when Johnstone reported finding a channel from the strait to the ocean. Then, to add to his joy, the Spanish decided to explore on their own!

Meeting a trading brig in the channel to the ocean, Vancouver learned from the captain that the *Daedalus* was at Nootka and that Quadra was impatient. He abandoned his survey and followed the coast to Nootka Sound.

5

In his journal Matt wrote of being entertained at a whale blubber feast at the home of Maquinna, who proudly displayed four wives and fifty slaves. He described the whaling industry and a hideous celebration in which Maquinna sacrificed a slave and laid his body side by side with the head of a whale.

During the weeks he negotiated with Quadra,

Vancouver often invited Matt to accompany him. Both Matt and the mate who served as interpreter wondered at the warm relationship developing between Vancouver and Quadra – unusual because Spain and England were traditional enemies, and because Vancouver harboured deep resentment of Spanish explorers. Whispers spread about the bond, so close that Vancouver and Quadra named the island Vancouver had circuited the "Island of Quadra and Vancouver" (later, Vancouver Island).

The friendship of Vancouver and Quadra did not enable them to agree on sovereignty. They decided to shelve the issue until their governments reached a decision.

Heading south, Vancouver assigned a survey of the Columbia River to Broughton, who made a landfall at Point Vancouver (now Vancouver, WA) and concluded that the river was not the Northwest Passage.

Vancouver sent Broughton to Mexico and on to England with dispatches and promoted Puget to command of the *Chatham*. He returned to the Sandwich Islands for the 1792 winter.

In 1793 Vancouver examined Dean's Channel one month before Alexander Mackenzie reached that site after traversing the continent. His health was failing. After he completed a survey of the Alaskan coast, he headed for England.

At a third Nootka Convention in Madrid, Spain and England agreed that neither would maintain a base at Nootka, and that they would prevent other countries from doing so.

6

Matt stayed aboard the *Discovery* until the crew dropped anchor in the Thames. He had hoped in vain that

Vancouver would return to Burrard Inlet where he might see Kah-te.

Matt received a long-overdue commission, and he thought seriously of a Royal Navy career. His family urged him to consider education or the business world. Pondering his resolve to return to Kah-te, he smarted with indecision. He relaxed to the comforts of home, however, and procrastinated about making a choice. Then his father died, and by necessity he assumed management of the family business. When he thought of Kah-te and wondered about the child she had promised, he romanticized about a son, and he felt guilt. Slowly, though, the idea of life with her became less realistic until it faded into a beautiful memory, which he rarely summoned to mind. In time, he succeeded in his career, married well, and fathered two sons.

In his first years at home Matt continued his association with George Vancouver, who suffered from kidney failure. Sadly, too, he followed some distressing accusations laid against Vancouver. In the notorious Camelford Affair, the unruly Thomas Pitt – Baron Camelford by then – charged Vancouver with subjecting him to flogging and shackles. Pitt also accused Vancouver of having discharged him for unacceptable conduct at a time when he had inherited membership in the House of Lords. Acting almost deranged at times, he challenged Vancouver to a duel.

Vancouver requested placing his problem before a tribunal of Admiralty naval officers but was denied that permission. When Matt heard allegations of Vancouver's brutality, he was so incensed that he stated publicly, "Strict he was and guilty of outbursts, which were frightening, but brutal – never!" Other officers joined Matt to attest to Vancouver's concern for his men's health and safety. They agreed that Pitt was troublesome and deserved his punishments.

Afterward, Vancouver put his arms about Matt and hugged him warmly. "Thank you, my son," he murmured, tears in his eyes.

Matt would always remember that show of affection from the man he cared for deeply. News of George Vancouver's death grieved but did not surprise him. What a tragedy, he sorrowed, for this fine man to die at the age of forty without acclamation for his immense contribution to his country! But he rejoiced that Vancouver lived to read proofs of his *Voyage of Discovery to the North Pacific Ocean and Around the World,* published after his death by his brother and Captain Peter Puget.

CHAPTER XIII

For Kah-te the glory of her night of love did not dim, and she clung to its memory. The boats had returned once – the time Kwamu prevented her reaching them – so she reasoned that they would come again. Over and over she whispered, *"tel-cha,"* the name she had given Matt, as if her longing would draw him to her. She often took from hiding the gold horseshoe he had given her and wet it with her tears. Convinced that she was bearing his child, she avoided facing the complications that pregnancy would entail for her. She was confident that Matt would save her.

Kah-te's immediate concern was for Tahulet, frightened as she approached childbirth because her pregnancy had been difficult. Kah-te tried to allay Tahulet's fear, and she chided Luhk for his lack of concern.

Because of Kwamu's importance, Tahulet received special care. She was carrying Kwamu's first grandchild, who, if male, probably would be *sia'm* himself. After the shaman decided the baby was a boy, he tried to assure a perfect fetus. "Sleep on an arrow," he ordered.

Tahulet's distress was so noticeable that Kwamu hired four midwives with *siwcn*. They anticipated a hard delivery.

"The family cares about the baby, not me," Tahulet said to Kah-te.

"The baby will bring your husband close," soothed Kah-te.

When labour pains began, Tahulet's joy of being pregnant disappeared. Slaves enclosed the fire pit she and Luhk shared, and the midwives whisked her inside.

Luhk shuddered at Tahulet's moans and walked in the woods. He had given little thought to being a father. Recalling Kah-te's scolding, he felt remorse for having shown so little sympathy.

The attendants put Tahulet on a mat, spread her hair on her shoulders, oiled her body, and stroked her abdomen each time she cried out with pain.

Tahulet strained and shrieked as her contractions became agonizing. Not comprehending her complications, the midwives tried to minimize them by jiggling dried deer toes and sprinkling Tahulet with down. At long last, they manipulated the fetus and delivered a boy. They wrapped the umbilical cord in goat's wool to prevent simple-mindedness in the baby.

The shaman returned to paint Tahulet's face and massage her again. The dancers followed to wash and oil the baby.

Still faint, Tahulet struggled against the throbbing in her body and the torturous ministrations of the midwives, who bound her abdomen with cedar wrappings and applied hot poultices to her breasts to "cook" her milk.

When the dancers left, one midwife wrapped the baby's legs – to straighten them while soft – and swaddled him in absorbent matting; she laced him in a cradle and put a clam shell against his lips for sucking until such time as she thought nursing would be suitable. Two midwives and Luhk carried the afterbirth to the woods and buried it for the protection of Tahulet and the baby.

After the midwives departed, laden with blankets as pay, Luhk edged into the enclosure and looked down at Tahulet, who reclined by the fire. He dropped to his knees beside the cradle and fell in love with his son. He grinned with pride and affection.

To Tahulet, Luhk's smile was worth the long labour. She chafed under the corset and breast pads, but she felt joyous and looked forward to enforced confinement with Luhk and the baby.

During the seclusion Luhk tended the fire and prepared food. When the baby cried, he crooned and placed him against Tahulet to nurse. Together he and Tahulet bathed their son, changing the mattress when he soiled it, and enjoyed him. The confinement was happy for both of them.

At a birth feast the shaman pierced the baby's ears, fastened bands to begin shaping his head, laced down his arms, and attached a hollow tube to divert his urine to the foot of the cradle. Tahulet could cuddle her son only when she bathed or nursed him; she carried the cradle on her back.

One day Luhk said, "As father I will hold a naming ceremony and give blankets. My father will give a name from an ancestor."

"My father will give a name, too," said Tahulet.

At the ceremony both grandfathers pledged to add more names at the boy's puberty and marriage.

Paw-neset said, "When I die, my name will go. Take it now."

"We'll save the sire names and call him Kwahl," Luhk said in his gentle way. "'Born to be,' it means. Born to be joy."

2

Kah-te patted her slightly rounded abdomen and rejoiced that she bore the child of her lover. Still hoping for a future with Matt, she continued to ignore her danger, but she admitted that he might not return soon enough to save her.

The danger that Kah-te faced was that Kwamu could kill her baby at birth if the shaman considered it a bastard or suspected that an outsider had fathered it; he could execute her as well. Were she not a slave, she could give blankets to cleanse herself and the baby of illegitimacy.

Until the birth Kah-te felt safe, because Kwamu assumed he had sired her child and would take no action. He had laid his hand on her and scowled, but she saw him strut away as if proud of his achievement. Maybe he doesn't know about such things or doesn't remember trading me for one night, she thought. The older slave women urged Kah-te to marry a slave and save herself. Or press against a digging stick to kill the baby. Or kill herself! Slaht, a kind slave, offered to marry her. First I'll try another way, she decided. I'll charm Kwamu.

Planning her strategy, Kah-te stepped into the woods when she knew Kwamu was watching and, as she hoped, he followed. She headed for a grassy alder grove and pretended to look for berries, making herself vulnerable and showing surprise when he approached and pushed her down. But this time, instead of tolerating his attack without emotion, she embraced and fondled him in the manner she had made love with Matt. She hated every moment, but she feigned pleasure and provided Kwamu with an ecstasy new to him. Afterward, she spoke of her desire to satisfy him, but she was careful that he did not suspect her motive. She drew his hand to her abdomen and smiled into his eyes.

While Kwamu rested, partially unclothed and still sprawled on her, Kahte noticed Luhk, who had happened upon them. He stood in the shadows with his mouth agape. Then he fled.

To Kwamu, Luhk's discovering them meant nothing, because it was natural for a master to fornicate with his slaves. He was unaware of Luhk's affection for Kah-te.

Later, when Luhk accosted Kah-te, she was unprepared for the extent of his reaction. "You and my father!" he stormed. "And . . . and you . . . you enjoyed it!"

"You forget that I am his slave . . . I do what he says. You have a wife. You don't need me."

"I want you." Luhk dropped his head. "My father . . . you will have his child, but I'll marry you even so." Then, realizing Kah-te's danger, he exclaimed, "He could order your death! I'll fight him!"

"No!" Kah-te cried. "It will be more dangerous if he's angry. Just ask for mercy. My friend, go to your wife and baby. Be happy."

Luhk stood tall. "The day will come when you'll be mine," he said confidently. "I promise! But now, you must marry a slave and save your life. Will you do that, Kah-te?"

"I'll think about it."

3

Paw-neset died that fall; the shaman could not save him.

Four persons with *siwcn* washed the corpse, bound it in a crouching position, and placed it in a square coffin. After the *Sxwaixwe* dancers backed in four times, chanting a doleful song, the family carried the box to an elevated grave house. Kwamu and Luhk beat their breasts in despair, and male guests, simulating ghosts, danced and whipped torches back and forth to purify the family and banish Pawneset's ghost from Kwamu's house.

Kwamu was distraught because he must do without his father's advice and must take over instructing the young. Luhk grieved that with his grandfather gone he must assume full manhood. The death worried Kah-te, for she knew that slave-selling was a common method of defraying funeral expenses. Fortunately, though, mourners contributed costs.

4

Nearing term, Kah-te was not surprised when Kwamu tired of her because he found their sexual activity uncomfortable. He became antagonistic and struck her several times.

"You must marry a slave!" Luhk cried.

In desperation Kah-te married Slaht and moved her mat beside his. The ceremony consisted of exchanging blankets and providing a meal for the other slaves.

Slaht was twenty years older than Kah-te. He never had dared court her when she obviously was their master's favourite. He was a meek man but jolly and caring. He marvelled at his good fortune, and he promised to care for Kah-te and consider her child as his own.

Kah-te winced when she thought of submitting to the sexual wants of both Kwamu and Slaht, desiring neither. But I'll be safe, she consoled herself, and maybe I'll care for Slaht.

When Kah-te's labour began, she and Slaht retreated to a shed he built in the woods, because a slave could not give birth in the house. For Kah-te there were no dancers or midwives. A slave woman went with them to help her.

As her labour progressed, Kah-te groaned, sweated, and, with an extreme push, gave birth to a boy. Quickly, the woman shook him until he cried and handed him to Slaht, who was faint from watching the birth.

"Take him, dolt! More! Ay-eee . . . another one!"

Writhing with one more effort, Kah-te delivered a second child, a girl. Twins! Laughing, she rose on one elbow to see her babies. She was incredulous of the wailing pair.

As she washed and wrapped the babies, the slave woman was speechless with awe. Kah-te and Slaht looked at them with the same astonishment. For both babies had skin lighter than Stalo colouring, and the girl's hair had a red tint!

"Ay-eee! Spirits!" cried the woman. "Twins, and strange looking, too!" Fearful of spirit power, she thrust the after-births at Slaht. "Bury deep!" she ordered.

Kah-te concentrated on the wee infants, whom she put to her breasts. I alone know the reason for their colour, she told herself. Kwamu did not see my *tel-cha's* hair. But he still will punish me if he suspects an outsider. What will he think about twins?

Slaht knelt beside Kah-te. "What will you name them?" he asked.

"My son . . . our son, Kukutwam. Squamish word I learned. Means 'waterfall.' Girl, Sehla . . . 'stars.'"

Slaht nodded. Unlike their masters, slaves were allowed names at birth. Kah-te had chosen names suggestive of her night of love, not imagining she would use both!

Kah-te was terrified that Kwamu would order her execution, and Slaht tried to comfort her. "Remember that these babies have *siwcn!*" he said.

There was a sound at the door and Kah-te trembled.

"I hear pebbles rattling in a shell! It's the shaman!" cried Slaht.

Kah-te clutched the babies to her. Was he coming to snatch them from her, possibly kill her?

To Kah-te and Slaht's amazement, the shaman entered and began to celebrate, dancing around them and sprinkling down! As he wailed to the spirits, they knew he meant to spare Kah-te's life and respect the babies because they were twins! And when he leaned over to inspect the babies, he painted their faces, a symbol of favour! The danger was over!

By order of the shaman, Kwamu visited with instructions. He was ill at ease, for he knew that Kah-te had become somewhat independent, and he recognized the spirit power of the babies.

With a joyous start Kah-te understood that if Kwamu suspected he had not fathered the twins, he would neither admit it nor admonish her; to be the father would be an honour! She sighed with relief – and with dismay when she realized that marrying Slaht had been unnecessary!

Keep the babies here for one moon," Kwamu said. "Pick up the boy first. Twins have special powers. So do parents."

Kah-te wondered if Kwamu were including himself as parent or referring to Slaht, whose presence he ignored as being unworthy of attention. "What power do parents have?" she asked demurely.

Eager to escape, Kwamu replied, "You, Kah-te, have the power to cure rheumatism by sucking sore parts. And you, husband, will have a vision."

When the seclusion ended, the shaman oiled Kah-te and Slaht, painted their faces, and led them to the village to parade with the babies.

Kwamu gave a feast and announced the powers of the twins to the village: "When the sea is stormy, we oil the boy's hair and dip him in the water to calm it. To stop rain, we burn a bit of twin hair. Later, as children, they can order weather." After whispering with the shaman, he continued. "Mahli people must guard these twins and their *siwcn,*" he said firmly. "Qals gave them different skin and hair, made them special. If a twin dies, his power is gone. The other twin will die of loneliness. Then we would lose *all* their power! We will protect them!"

PART III

The Blend

CHAPTER XIV

Matt Stewart leaned back in his armchair and smiled at his two sons as he raised *The Times* to turn the page. Ian, the younger, sprawled before the fireplace with his dog, and the reflecting flames accentuated red streaks in his hair. He lay on his side, scratching the dog's head.

Matt's elder son, David, stood beside Ian, hands clasped behind his back and eyes on Matt's face. He was a strong, slender youth, resembling neither his brother nor his father. A clump of dark, wavy hair fell on his brow, and his complexion was noticeably darker. "Father," he said, clearing his throat, "I'd like to . . . to discuss something."

"And what do you wish to discuss, son?" Matt asked kindly.

"I . . ," David stammered, "well, I . . . I don't want to return to classes next term!" Then his words came in a nervous rush. "I want to go to the colonies, to North America, and . . . and travel so I can write about those places."

Matt jerked straight in the chair. "You want to do what?"

"Actually, Father, I'd like to . . . to join the Hudson's Bay Company, to clerk in Canada and the Northwest!" David cowered a bit, aware of the impact of his words but glad to have said them after summoning courage to confront his father.

"And give up your education? You're an excellent student!"

"Father, I don't want to be a business man. I just want to write. You know that!"

"Yes, but you're only sixteen, my boy. You may discover you like other professions. Does your mother know about this?"

"No, I've kept it secret. Oh, Father, you think well of

the Hudson's Bay Company. Aren't you a shareholder or something like that? I know you go to their meetings in London."

"Well, yes, I do attend the annual meetings. I inherited my membership. But . . ."

"And when you were my age, didn't you want to do something different? You've told us about going to sea. Weren't you younger than I am?" David had rehearsed his campaign.

Matt hesitated, for David spoke the truth. His mind spun back, and his face revealed undisguised pleasure. He flushed, recalling the night with Kah-te; the memory had lain dormant for years.

David watched curiously; and Ian, who had been listening only halfheartedly, sat up expectantly.

Matt focused on the present. "You're right, David," he replied. "I was younger, but I've oft regretted giving up my education. I went into business when I left the sea, you know."

"But I can finish my education afterward!"

"Dear boy, I can use influence to get you an apprenticeship with the Hudson's Bay Company. But do you know you'd have to be a clerk for *eight* years before you could have any command? Do you really want that? You'd join as a so-called gentleman, but Canada's wild! A hard life even for an officer!"

"Wild country's what I want! Adventure! I can learn more by travel than at a university! I don't mind eight years. I'll write about things never printed before! Oh, please let me go, Father!"

Matt was silent. He saw himself thirty years before, appealing to *his* parents. He knew that he was not entirely truthful, for he always had considered his years at sea to be just as valuable as formal education. Cautiously he replied,

"I'll speak to your mother."

At David's urging Matt related more of his experiences in the Navy and told of the history of the Hudson's Bay Company. "Charles II founded the Company," he said, "after Henry Hudson discovered beaver dams by the thousand and started England's fur.trading. Rupert's Land, they called the colony."

"I've heard the Company has a lot of competition."

"You're right. A constant fight to hang on to its riches – competition with the French, the Indians, and the North West Company . . ."

"I'll like that, Father."

2

David joined the Hudson's Bay Company in 1814 as an apprenticed clerk at an annual salary of twenty pounds. He crossed the Atlantic on a supply ship and docked at York Factory on Hudson Bay, where he stayed many months before progressing to other Company stations. He served at Norway House, at Cumberland House, at a post in the Athabasca country, and at Fort Edmonton.

Most forts were similar: palisades with corner bastions enclosing a Chief Trader's residence, barracks, wash house, kitchen, forge, and trade shop.

Company life was rugged. David's duties were to trade with Indian trappers, oversee equipment, and take a turn tending crops or cleaning and pressing furs into bales. After evening meals with the officers, he updated his journal. He concentrated on a study of Indian habits and personalities, relishing every contact with natives. He described living conditions in the forts:

Without books or other diversions, some men console

themselves by trading buttons and tobacco for native mistress-
es. For pleasure I often go with the French Canadian
voyageurs in their birch-bark York boats, as they haul supplies
west and return with rawhide, dressed leather, and ninety-
pound bales of pelts. Eight tough men operate each boat –
tough enough to portage the boat and cargo overland.

On holidays, when the Chief Trader usually condones
feasting and drinking, I see confusion among the Indians
whom we invite to party with us. I wonder at the wisdom of
offering them liquor.

When David's eight-year apprenticeship ended, the
Company offered him a contract as an accountant or a
post commander. He would be required to serve three
more years, however, to earn a Chief Trader commission.
Eager to edit and publish his journals, which bulged with
notes and stories, he disliked so long a wait. So, taking
advantage of the fact that the Company was reducing staff
and would not object to his leaving, he resigned and
returned to England in 1821.

3

Before 1810 the Hudson's Bay Company had made
only minor advances beyond the Rocky Mountains. The
North West Company, on the other hand, founded trading posts in western territory, which Simon Fraser named
New Caledonia. An attempt by the Hudson's Bay
Company to infringe on the western trade resulted in
ambushes of rival forts. Almost bankrupt, the two com-
panies settled their battle for power soon after David
returned to England. They amalgamated as the new
Hudson's Bay Company. A London committee would control the entire fur trade west of the Rockies.

As governor of New Caledonia, the Company appointed George Simpson, a young clerk so dynamic that he became known as the "Little Emperor" of the fur trade.

English peddlers, Simpson discovered, had rarely appeared in Pacific coastal waters after the demise of the sea otter trade. Americans, however, routinely negotiated with the Indians for furs, which they sold for high prices in China and then loaded silk, spices, and porcelain for profit on their return to America. He decided that the Hudson's Bay Company should draw England back into the maritime fur trade. To strengthen British presence on the Columbia River, he built Fort Vancouver; from there the New Caledonia posts could ship furs east by a vast chain of waterways and portages known as "the Communication."

David wondered if his resignation was ill-timed, because the merger would enable him to go to the Northwest. So he published his journals, then eagerly accepted a commission to investigate and write about the natives of the Pacific coast.

Matt had been in failing health for several years, and David had misgivings about leaving him. At his bedside, Matt pressed David's hand. "My son," he said weakly, "I understand your need to go. I had it once, and I . . . I've always wanted to return. Now your study of Indians reminds me of . . . of something Captain Vancouver said. It sounded strange then but . . . but maybe now. . . ."

"Tell me, Father."

"He thought white man had harmed, not helped the Indians!"

"I'll remember that."

Matt closed his eyes, his energy fading, but opened them and went on. "I . . . I wanted to go back to . . . to one place above all. A place Vancouver explored. Burrard

Inlet, it's called." Breathing hard, Matt struggled with baring his long-kept secret. Haltingly, he said, "There was . . . there was an Indian girl . . . I've never forgotten her."

David listened to his father with awe at his intense emotion. "And you want me to find this girl, Father?"

"Well, er . . . yes, the girl who . . . who knew the English sailor. Tell her I . . . I remember her. But . . . but you won't speak of this to anyone . . ."

David nodded. "No, not to my mother and not to Ian. And I'll look for your beautiful Indian maiden. I'm sure there's a story here but that's all you're going to tell me. Am I right?"

Matt smiled and wearily closed his eyes again.

With Hudson's Bay Company consent David sailed from England in 1827 on the *Cadboro,* a new schooner that Britain commissioned as a supply vessel for Fort Vancouver.

4

One year earlier, George Simpson had become "Governor in Chief, Hudson's Bay Company Territory," managing operations from Hudson Bay to the Pacific. He hoped to seize fur trade control from the Americans – the hated "Boston men," as the Indians called them. He wanted a supply route north of the suggested international boundary at 49 degrees latitide, and he decided to establish Fort Langley on the Fraser River.

David accompanied the men who sailed up the Fraser in July 1827 on the *Cadboro* to build and staff Fort Langley at a site where the ship could draw close to the bank.

The river seemed to bulge with Indians, as hundreds headed upriver for the *tsukai* run. Some wanted to trade, others to terrorize. But Kwantlen Indians living near the fort watched the building quietly; their *sia'ms* offered friendship with gifts of salmon, berries, and hazelnuts.

Trappers, traders, and Company men found communicating with Indians relatively easy because, like the explorer Captain John Meares, they learned the trade jargon. Bit by bit they added words, simplified it phonetically, and adopted gestures for emphasis. The vocabulary consisted of about five hundred words; men could converse with a few dozen important words and could learn the entire vocabulary in several weeks. The jargon became known as Chinook.

5

Being in the Company without assigned duties was a new experience for David. Some of the men did not understand his independence, or that writing could be a career; but he was popular, and the men regarded him as an equal.

English, Scottish, French Canadian, and Kanaka – Hawaiian natives from early trading ships – were as one, and David laboured with them. Together, they cleared ground, cut timber, and carved pickets. Many men fell ill from their diet – primarily salmon – and from exposure to incessant rainy weather.

In November Chief Trader Archibald McDonald raised a flag above Fort Langley, which the Indians called Snugamish. Measuring less than half an acre, the stockade included two-story blockhouses fitted with cannons and gunports.

Though he was at liberty to frequent any Company post, David stayed at Fort Langley. Finding new material daily, he made detailed entries in his journal, some of trivial events and some of more dramatic happenings such as a minor earthquake, a forest fire set by antagonistic natives, and a downpour that put out the flames like an answered prayer. He wrote of gloomy days filled with mud, mire, and monotony; of the joyous receipt of mail; and of All Saints' Day, Christmas, and New Year's Day when celebrations boosted morale.

I want to concentrate on writing about Indians rather than the Company, David reminded himself. But I need personal contact to study Indian life. Beyond the fort. Somehow, I must find it.

CHAPTER XV

At Mahli Kah-te still watched expectantly when ships were in sight, but most passed offshore. Though rescue was unnecessary after the birth of twins changed her life, she clung to hope over the years that Matt would return.

She sped to the riverbank when she saw the *Cadboro.* That Matt's son was aboard was beyond fantasy!

She thought of the time whiteman [Simon Fraser] had landed at Musqueam, the village above Mahli. She was visiting there that day. Mistaking Fraser for an enemy, the men had hidden in trees, so that he saw only women and children. After he explored, Fraser discovered that an ebbing tide had grounded his boats. Then the Musqueam sprang from hiding, "howling like so many wolves and brandishing war clubs," he reported. Breaking away, Fraser took a hasty look at Mahli and the sea, then headed upstream, having concluded that the river was not a satisfactory route to the Pacific.

Kah-te recalled something else about that day. One whiteman had eyed her with interest, and he had reddish hair! But he was not her *tel-cha.* Her yen to see Matt again, she realized, was less to revive youthful passion than to satisfy her curiosity. She wondered how he would look.

As the *Cadboro* moved upriver, Kah-te glanced at the fishing activity before her – the river swarming with canoes and the shore with men tending weirs and women processing fish. As a slave she had duties, but her elevated position protected her from reprimand when she preferred not to work. She saw her daughter Sehla cutting salmon with the women; Kukutwam, Sehla's twin, was with the fishermen.

There are fewer *tsukai* this year, and enough workers,

Kah-te told herself. I'm old and not well. I'll rest. The ship makes me remember. So much has happened since that night . . . so much since my twins were born.

2

Kwamu had provided Kah-te and Slaht with their own fire pit in his house, and he allowed Kah-te to care for the babies of her own free will. She still was his slave, as were the twins, but common belief that Kwamu was the father gave her status. Kah-te and the babies also had *siwcn,* affording them privileges, and the village guarded safety of the twins.

Kah-te's life had been pleasant when her children were small. Slaht was helpful, and she was fond of him, though she cringed when he came to her mat. He was so worship-ful of her, in fact, that he had little control of his emotion when he lay with her, and his potency diminished quickly.

On the surface, Kah-te's relationship with Kwamu did not change. He could not profess to have sired the chil-dren, though she knew he prided himself as the father. Because of her status, she could disobey any order without much fear, but she could not deny her body to her master. However, with Slaht and the babies sleeping beside her, it was inconvenient for Kwamu to visit her mat, and she avoided him in the woods.

Several times Kwamu ordered Kah-te to meet him, but there was a difference in their procedure. When she was bargaining for her life, she had pleased him to excess, but after the birth she offered only dutiful response. Her spir-ituality also subdued him. More and more he satisfied himself with his wives and other slaves.

Then came smallpox, twenty years after it last had spread its ravages. It swept through the river valley with a frightening death toll. Kah-te recalled abject fear when several persons in Mahli broke out.

Kwamu asked eight-year-old Kukutwam to lay his hand on a stricken woman and hope to cure her with his *siwcn*. Two weeks later, Kukutwam was nauseous and whimpered with pain. Red blotches appeared on his forehead. He was fiery with fever.

Kah-te rocked Kukutwam and soothed him with cool pads. She crooned lullabies and cried softly as he seemed to slip away from her. The shaman pranced around him many hours of each day; it was important for this child with the *siwcn* to live! As nothing was known of contagion, Slaht and Sehla hovered nearby.

Kukutwam survived, with relatively few pitted scars, and miraculously, Kah-te, Slaht, and Sehla did not become infected.

Others in the village were not so fortunate. Kwamu was the most renowned victim; all the shaman's healing efforts failed for the *sia'm* of Mahli.

Kah-te adjusted to Kwamu's death with difficulty. Except for freedom from his sexual demands, she missed him, for he usually was good to her. She now belonged to Luhk, who became *sia'm* and inherited Kwamu's slaves.

3

After the birth of his son Kwahl, Luhk had regarded his marriage with more enthusiasm. Tahulet reasoned that if Kwahl's birth had endeared her to Luhk, she surely should have more children. His affection would be worth enduring the horrible birth procedure again!

Kwamu's death distressed Atsaian. He was uneasy about his relationship with Luhk as *sia'm*, who not only was young but was his son-in-law. When he arrived at the river for the next *tsukai* season, however, he went to Mahli and sought out Luhk and Tahulet. With him he had a toddler, a boy slightly older than Kwahl. "I bring a friend," he said, thrusting the child forward. "His name is Ki-ap-a-la-no. He needs a home."

"Why is that?" asked Luhk.

"His father was Squamish, his mother Musqueam. Both died of pox. My wives are too old to raise him. My tyee, Te Kiapalanoq, wants Musqueam to raise him. I ask you to take him as your own."

"My father, you offer this boy to my husband and me?" Tahulet asked with delight.

"I'll tell why I chose you. The boy's father, Cheatmuh, is a son of Te Kiapalonoq. The Squamish have an old belief that Cheatmuh was also the son of Kalana, First Man of the Squamish. I won't say more..."

Luhk broke in. "Sire! This child will become an important man?"

"Take him. You'll be glad."

"This boy needs us – that's reason enough for us to take him. Does my wife want him?"

Tahulet looked longingly at Ki-ap-a-la-no and reached out her arms. She had become a capable mother, hoping in vain for more children. "Ay, my husband," she replied happily.

So Ki-ap-a-la-no became a foster child of Luhk and Tahulet, who loved him and raised him with Kwahl and three children they had later. But, recalling Atsaian's prediction, they were not surprised when the Squamish tyee ordered Ki-ap-a-la-no's return to Homulchesen. He had grown to an impressive height with a deep voice and straight hair hanging to his shoulders. He was wise, and he had adopted much of Luhk's honesty and decency.

4

As young as he was when he assumed his father's duties as *sia'm*, Luhk was a dependable, efficient leader. His dearest trait, to Kah-te, was his compassion – he felt the sorrows of others as his own. He abhorred war; and he still grieved about having killed a man and captured helpless women and children during the raid on the Euclataw. His pacifism became an obsession.

Kah-te was glad that Luhk had stopped speaking of his feeling for her, though he often confided problems. *Maybe he remembers urging me to marry Slaht. Or maybe Luhk doesn't like my rank,* she contemplated. *Or maybe he believes my twins are his half-brother and sister, because he saw me with his father.* She was quick to congratulate him on the birth of each of his children, to encourage him in raising Ki-ap-a-la-no, and to praise Tahulet to him at every opportunity.

Unexpectedly, Slaht died of dysentery. Soon afterward, Luhk followed Kah-te to the woods when she went to bathe in the creek. He approached her with a smile.

"Dear Kah-te," he said, "The time has come for me to raise your rank and make you my wife. Would you like that?"

"Oh, master," Kah-te replied, "you have a wife! One is enough!"

"But I love you. We're already kin – your children and I have the same father. And I need you."

Kah-te interrupted. "Your wife is my friend. She loves you. I don't want to hurt her!"

"I can take any wife I want. My wife will say nothing."

"Oh, master, she would not want you to take me!"

"Wives expect that."

To Kah-te Luhk's words sounded as if his father spoke

them. But he pulled her to him, not with demand, but tenderly. "Kah-te, lie with me," he said. "I'll make you happy."

Kah-te could close her eyes and believe she was with her *tel-cha,* the only other person who had been concerned with making her happy. Yet here was this man who could take her without asking, this man offering to please her with his body, raise her rank, and marry her. She relaxed against Luhk. As he gently aroused her, she was helpless to temptation. She surrendered to the exciting emotion, and she relived the only caring lovemaking she had known.

Luhk waited for an appropriate time, called the people of Mahli together, and made speeches in Kah-te's honour, giving away blankets and offering a feast to his guests. "To wipe away the stain of being a slave. To take her as my wife," he announced. He arranged for Kah-te to move her fire near Tahulet's so he would be free to dine or sleep with either one.

In her naïveté Tahulet never had noticed Luhk's interest in Kah-te. She wept with distress but soon accepted the situation.

5

Kah-te shook her head as if to clear it of the past and return to reality. Slowly, she strolled to the rocks where the women were preparing salmon. It would be pleasant to work beside Sehla and speculate about the ship, which had faded out of sight.

CHAPTER XVI

Several weeks after the *Cadboro* passed Mahli, Luhk said, "There's whiteman trouble upriver. I'm going there."

"I'll go, too," volunteered Kwahl.

"And I," eagerly added Kukutwam. "I'm lonely here. Kwahl is usually busy with his family and Ki-ap-a-la-no has gone to the Squamish." The three young men were close friends.

"You don't *have* to be lonely!" chided Kwahl, smiling.

"I'm glad you both want to go," said Luhk.

To Luhk's dismay a troublesome band of men from Musqueam pulled into the stream as he started upriver with Kwahl and Kukutwam. He approached Fort Langley with trepidation.

From the fort David observed them: in particular Luhk, earnestly offering dried salmon, and Kukutwam, whose skin was light and pockmarked. When David smiled, Kukutwam nodded in reply, but there was no chance for talk. The Musqueam band had become boisterous, arguing loudly that Boston men paid more for beaver pelts. Luhk cut the visit short to avoid a fracas.

2

David read part of a speech by Governor Simpson: *"These treacherous savages respect us in proportion to our strength and means of defense."*

Enraged, David wrote to the governor:

Sir! I beg to differ with you. The Indians are not treacherous savages! I resent your attitude. You claim to respect the Indians but label them as wretched and dishonest. You believe in ruling with a rod of iron and try to make them fear us —

to prevent trouble, you say. You tell us not to become too familiar because the natives mistake kindness for cowardice. I do not agree!

In his journal he listed more concerns:

Natives come here in swarms, and Fort Langley is changing. The Kwantlen have supplied us with hundreds of skins. But alas, they've discovered that they can have luxuries in exchange for their skins! They've been too obsessed with trapping beaver to dry fish and berries. They're neglecting their own people! Their children are hungry in this land of plenty! The Indian kills only what he needs; mass slaughter of fur-bearing animals is contrary to his belief. Worse still, this winter is severe, but the Indians have peddled all their furs. They're cold and bargaining for blankets. They're pitiful for another reason — our blankets are drab, but they weave beautiful ones.

I'm bothered that our men take Indian wives, then head back east and abandon both wives and half-breed babies.

3

The time has come for a change, David decided. If I want to observe Indian life, I must leave the fort. Perhaps I'll go to Burrard Inlet where my father met the Indian girl — I feel guilty that I've not been there. He smiled, still intrigued that his staid father had "sown some wild oats."

"Too dangerous," the officers said. "Many Indians are unfriendly and the river can be tricky this time of year."

"Maybe kindness will be enough of a weapon," David replied. "I'm not afraid."

In the spring he bought a small canoe, stocked it with provisions and trade articles, and set out downriver. He consented to taking a musket and powder flask.

For a few days he paddled slowly, travelling with the current at favourable tides. Occasionally he beached to explore plant life. Most villages welcomed him, though he guarded his equipment. He camped each night, building a fire and cooking a fish when he could hook one. With hand movements and Chinook he conversed with the Indians amazingly well. He made copious notes.

One night, after he had prepared supper and was dozing by the fire, a band of Cowichans stalked and attacked him. Coveting his gun in particular, they took all of his possessions. With no desire for a white slave, they hacked at him with harpoons. Whiteman will blame the Musqueam, they decided, if the body is found downriver – or washed out to sea and never found. They dumped David into his canoe, removed the oars, and pushed the boat into midstream.

David lay face down, bleeding and unconscious. He drifted all night and into the next day. Rain beat on him, and mist obscured his canoe from observation on shore. He roused once and tried to clear crusted blood from his eyes. Weak from loss of blood, he fainted again.

At dusk, when the fog lifted, Kukutwam was paddling to Mahli from the opposite bank, battling a strong tide. When he spied David's canoe, he drew alongside, then towed it to the village. Leaping out, he carried David to the longhouse. *"My ta'ta!"* he called to his mother, "Help me!"

David was near death. Kah-te and Sehla bathed the gashes on his body, poulticing and binding them with herbs. He groaned, and when he opened his eyes for a moment, Kah-te held water to his lips. The shaman pirouetted and blew on the wounds.

Luhk returned that evening from a village beyond Ulksn. He commended his family for helping a stranger.

"We saw this man at the fort," he said, "several moons ago."

"Ay," said Kukutwam.

As Kah-te was feeling unwell, Sehla tended David. She moved her mat beside him, wakening to every thrashing movement of his delirium and treating him with all the potions her people knew.

When the fever receded and David became conscious, Sehla's brown eyes sparkled with pleasure.

David blinked in wonder at Sehla, for she was a naturally beautiful woman with a lovely body. Kukutwam and Sehla had normal features because Kwamu had denied head flattening to them. As David had seen children of mixed parentage at the fort, Sehla's colouring did not seem unusual. Obviously she had a white father – a Scot, he guessed, because of the red in her hair.

David recognized Kukutwam. What a coincidence, he thought, for him to rescue me – or was it destiny that I meet his sister? And Sehla, holding David to offer sips of broth, was sure Kukutwam had found him and she had cured him because of their *siwcn*.

As David grew stronger, he basked in the goodness of the Musqueam people. Their animistic faith and oneness with nature appealed to him. In his journal he wrote:

They are dignified and honourable. They can be eloquent, even in Chinook. They refrain from insult. I've heard men at the fort say that the Indian shows no emotion, not even anger, and that he rarely expresses joy or sympathy. But I've learned to recognize a silent language – almost unobservable movements and changes in countenance. Among themselves, moreover, they chatter at length.

David's hair and beard grew long. When Kukutwam gave him a breechclout, moccasins, and deerhide tunic,

Sehla laughed. "You look Musqueam," she said.

"I *feel* like one of you," David replied. I'd like to live with these people for a while, he decided. I'm happy here. I'm finding purpose to my life for the first time. Sehla and Kukutwam are loving and sincere. And Luhk is one of the finest persons I've ever known.

"I want to write," he explained to Luhk, struggling with Chinook words and pointing to his journals. "I'll do chores for my keep." He thought it unwise to mention writing about Indian customs for publication.

"You stay. *Sikhs* [friend]. As long as you want."

4

As he observed the Indians at Mahli, David discovered Christian elements in many of their beliefs and ceremonies, and parallels between some of their legends and stories of the Bible. Their deity was called Saghalie Tyee in Chinook. It was as if the Indians had advance notice of Christianity long before the white man came. He had talks with Luhk about it.

"A'lias tell us what will happen. They say that white-man riches are evil for the Indian."

David recalled Captain Vancouver's remark that his father had repeated – of the damage done to the Indian by white men. His own misgivings were accumulating rapidly.

Luhk was an extraordinary *sia'm*. Unlike his aggressive father, Kwamu, he was humble, often exhibiting qualities that David called Christlike. His spirituality was his entire being; he lived by ethical rules and respected all living creatures. Though his preference for Kah-te was obvious, he was happy with Tahulet and honoured her as the mother of his children.

David became Luhk's confidant and Kukutwam's close

friend. And he fell in love with Sehla. I love her enough to make any sacrifice, he told himself, but is it wise to marry her? Have half-breed children? At Fort Langley he discussed his dilemma.

"Take a wife if you want, Stewart," the officers advised, "but live with her here at the fort. Don't bury yourself in a filthy Indian village!"

"Bury myself? Not at all," David replied defensively. "The Musqueam people have values that put some of ours to shame. I find purpose being with them. And . . . I love Sehla."

David concluded that he would be happy at Mahli, perhaps with an occasional visit to England. He married Sehla in a Musqueam ritual with four days of feasting and Sxwaixwe dancing. He participated fully and distributed blankets, ignoring censure of the practice by white clergy. Luhk welcomed David as a son-in-law and gave the newlyweds a fire pit of their own.

In the next few years David rarely looked back. He was content. He learned the Halkomelem language, and Musqueam ways became his. He wrote of their ceremonies and philosophy, periodically shipping his manuscripts from Fort Langley.

5

Soon after Sehla gave birth to a third child, Kah-te became gravely ill. Luhk and her small family gathered about her.

"Dear . . . husband," Kah-te said softly to Luhk. Reaching to her children, her voice faded to a whisper. "Kukutwam, beside a waterfall with my *tel-cha,* my lover . . . Sehla, under the stars," she said. Then she took Sehla's hand and dropped into it a small gold horseshoe. "From my *tel-cha* . . . He . . . he's your father." Joyous with remembrance, Kah-te died smiling.

Luhk bowed his head both in grief and surprise at Kah-te's revelation. As Sehla and Kukutwam wept and hugged her body, the charm fell to the floor.

David picked up the horseshoe, polished the front with his thumb, and turned it over. There was a mark – initials: *M.C.S.* For a few seconds the inscription had no meaning. Then all at once it was clear: M.C.S. – Matthew Chamberlain Stewart – my father! Kah-te is my father's Indian girl! Never did I imagine she would be anywhere but Burrard Inlet. When Father met her, she must have been visiting there, as the Indian people do for weddings and the like. Then his face went ashen. So . . . so then . . . *Sehla is my half-sister!*

Shock swept over David in a wave of nausea, and he went through the motions of grieving for Kah-te without feeling. Stalwart Anglican morals were ingrained in his being. I'm guilty of incest, he despaired. How can I tell Sehla . . . what future do our children have . . . what shall I do? I need help! I've sinned. I must leave Sehla and my dear children!

After the funeral, David tried to explain the situation to Sehla, but she did not understand and wept hysterically when he left. Luhk could see nothing harmful in his remaining, nor could Kukutwam; their eyes filled with hurt that he was forsaking all of them.

"I'll seek advice and hope to come back soon," David told them, but he knew that he would not.

6

David moved to Fort Langley and contemplated rejoining the Company or returning to England. Oddly, he told himself, I no longer think of England as home.

This land is my home; my family is here and these are my people. Yes, I want to stay here on the river. I want to be near my children and try to protect Sehla.

He longed to confide in clergy, to do penance for his sin, but no priests came that season. He found no help for his anguish or the tragedy ruining his life and Sehla's. Writing was his only consolation. Blanked of emotion, he functioned in a void, but he put together an article about Fort Langley's success in creating relative peace among the Stalo. He wrote:

Almost from the beginning, Indians harassed the fort with a war of nerves, because they didn't think we were brave enough to defend ourselves. Squaws, they called us, afraid to fight. But that notion came to an end when we decided to prove our mettle and terminate constant fear of the Euclataw.

All the river people feared the Euclataw. In one week we counted five hundred canoes with all kinds of booty, even human heads. Their canoes are too large to navigate in shallow water. I'm told they paddle as far as they can, then portage to remote villages where they loot and take slaves.

Fortunately, we had advance notice of a planned attack on the fort – and time to form our strategy. Our men waited as the enemy grouped to storm across the river and surprise us. When they were in range, we blasted them with a mighty barrage of gunfire. Canoes jammed with warriors exploded, splintered, and sank. Local Indians, waiting in the woods, leaped in to massacre the survivors; and we estimated that hundeds of Euclataw died in the attack. That should end their aggression!

Generally, Indians have accepted us and are copying some of our ways, such as cultivating fields. I'm not sure they should discard their own methods, but they've learned that growing potatoes is preferable to digging roots.

I alone know of my father's love affair, David told himself. I'm tempted to write of it, and it would be a profitable tale. It's much too personal for me to publish, but what spice it would add to the annals of the George Vancouver expedition!

David often reminded himself that his father had approved his marriage to Sehla, not knowing, of course, that she was his own daughter. How strange that I fulfill *his* dream! And what coincidence that I chose the daughter of his Kah-te from thousands of Indian women! *His* daughter!

Fort Langley came to be regarded as a major post, and the Company replaced it with a larger stockade several miles upstream, but fire destroyed the new fort a few months later. The third Fort Langley, where David was staying, provided for the fur trade, large-scale farming, and new industries. The fate of the fort hung briefly in the air, however, when the Company discussed unfavourable winds and tides at the river mouth that hindered navigation. The solution was the construction of the *Beaver,* a steam-engined vessel designed for shallow water. It could combat tides and wind, and would haul passengers and freight in a regular coastal circuit.

7

For the rest of his life David would remember the day he gloomily trudged to the dock as the *Beaver* approached. I can't escape from the bottomless pit I'm in, he told himself. There's only one way. It would be so easy to end it all . . ..

". . . and one for you, Stewart." When the clerk handed him an envelope, David glanced at it listlessly. London. From Ian, his brother. Strange . . . Ian rarely writes. With a spark of interest, David slit the envelope and pulled out the letter.

December 1830

Dear Brother:

It is my sad obligation to notify you that Father died today. As you know, he's been feeble for a long time. Mother cared for him while she could, but after her death he went downhill rapidly. I'll notify you later about your share of the estate. There will be some personal items for you, too, and you can advise me if you wish them sent.

You won't be pleased, but I must inform you of another matter, because I promised Father I would. He told me about it shortly before his death, and it's a lurid tale, hard to believe but true. It seems that our very proper mother was raped, if you can imagine, by a so-called trusted family counsellor. The man was quite old, and the husband of another victim later murdered the miserable devil! This happened after Mother and Father were engaged, and Father – always the valiant protector – insisted they go on with the wedding. He planned that not a soul ever would know of the rape or that Mother was pregnant from it. They told people their baby was premature. Their baby was not Father's, but they kept the secret well, telling no one, not even you. Yes, David, you had a different father, but I'm sure it doesn't matter, because Father always regarded you as his own, and as far as the estate goes
. . .

A different father!

David leaped up, waving the letter wildly. "A different father!" he shouted. "I'm not his son! Oh, Sehla, you're not my sister!"

Exultant with joy, David threw together his possessions and that day steamed downriver on the *Beaver's* return trip. For a fee the captain ordered a mate to put over a dinghy at Mahli and row David ashore. People stared as he raced up the bank and ducked into Luhk's lodge. "Sehla!" he shouted.

He met only blank stares. People in the house were expressionless, and Sehla was not at her fire.

Luhk stepped forward and grasped his hand. "You came," he said calmly.

"It's all right now, *Sia'm*. I had a letter. Sehla is not my sister! Where is she?"

"She's . . . not well," Luhk replied. "You left – you shamed her. She tried to end her life."

David saw her. "Sehla!" he cried, rushing to her. But there was no emotion on her face and she looked at him with unseeing eyes. She did not recognize him.

Luhk explained. "She swallowed poison berries. She does not speak."

Unbelievingly, David put his arms about Sehla. She was limp and unresponsive. Her lips curved in a meaningless smile. "What have I done? My precious Sehla! Oh, God," he wept. Then, turning to Luhk, he asked, "My children? Where are my children?"

"Kukutwam married and has them."

Tears spilled on David's cheeks. "I'll take care of Sehla," he said. "She'll get well. I know she will." Tenderly, he led her to a platform and bowed his head in distress.

8

Kukutwam blamed David for Sehla's condition and was slow to forgive him. However, he relinquished the children to David, offered to use his special twin *siwcn* as a cure, and encouraged David's effort to band his family together.

So earnest was David that others in the house tried to

help him. He often found his fire started, food prepared, or the children bathed. Gently, patiently, he nursed and pampered Sehla, never doubting that his love would cure her.

With genuine belief in the effectiveness of native ceremony, David asked the shaman to summon his healing powers. In full regalia the shaman danced about Sehla, sprinkled her with potions, and leaned close to her forehead to suck out the evil spirit clouding her mind.

In time, Sehla responded to David's care. One day she spoke his name, then gradually returned to reality. She was able to assume some responsibility, but her energy was limited and she did not fully recover mentally. David devoted himself to making her happy, supervising their children, performing his chores and hers, and satisfying her childlike whims.

CHAPTER XVII

When Ki-a-pa-la-no returned to Burrard Inlet, he was astonished to find it dormant – a contrast to the hubbub of the river valley. More than thirty years had elapsed since George Vancouver examined the inlet; except for a few trappers and Russian seal hunters, white men had not entered the Narrows again.

At Te Kiapalanoq's death, his tyee title went to Temlaham, his second son, because Cheatmuh, the first son and Ki-a-pa-lan-o's father, had died of pox.

"Son of my brother," Temlaham said to Ki-ap-a-la-no, "I summoned you because I have no son of my own. You will become *sia'm,* and you will take my place some day as Te Kiapalanoq."

Ki-ap-a-la-no gasped. "You want *me* to be Te Kiapalanoq, the tyee? But . . ."

"Do not worry. You are strong and your *sulia* will guide you. And I hope to live for many moons. Meanwhile, you must prepare – prove yourself."

"How . . . how do I do that?"

Temlaham paused, then spoke slowly. "We are at peace, but we live in fear. I speak for all the inlet people. We all fear."

"Fear of the Euclataw?"

"Ay, of another raid." Then Temlaham said, "Years ago Atsaian from Tlastlemauq led Squamish warriors to join the Musqueam in a strike on the Euclataw, but the Euclataw still attack us. Now we hear that whiteman on the river defeated the Euclataw – so soundly that the Euclataw never again will enter that river. They will spare the river people, but we in this inlet likely will be the victims!"

Ki-ap-a-la-no listened intently, knowing he should

make no comment while his uncle spoke. But he sensed a grave reason for the conversation.

"My nephew," Temlaham continued, "I want to win a battle like that in our waters so the Euclataw won't raid us again! We don't know whiteman because he doesn't come here. But you have been with him. You can show us his ways so we, too, can defeat the Euclataw!"

"But . . ."

Temlaham held up his hand. "Speak not. You'll find a way."

Ki-ap-a-la-no gulped, as his experience with whiteman was limited. He went into the forest to seek wisdom from his *sulia*. "My sire," he said, when he returned, *"A'lias* have told you that many whiteman will come, as on the river. These beautiful streams and forests are quiet now. But the river is not quiet. Whiteman changed it. He brought guns – magic sticks that make noise and spit fire. Whiteman killed the Euclataw and won victory with guns."

"We should use guns to fight?"

"In the woods for four days I thought about it. Ay, guns you need, evil guns. I can trade for some at Mahli – or my father can get them at the fort."

"So be it. Take rowers, skins, fish, whatever you need. I hope that you return in time."

2

A few months later Ki-ap-a-la-no was ready with a carefully devised scheme. He had rehearsed the people of Homulchesen. "We won't flee to the woods as usual," he had told them, "for if we do, they'll rob us again and take more women and children as slaves. No, this time we will fight!" He posted scouts at vantage points.

One day two scouts paddled furiously to

Homulchesen. "The Euclataw are coming!" they cried.

Quickly, several women followed directions and hurried to the beach where they busied themselves digging clams; they pretended not to notice the approaching Euclataw canoes until they were close. On cue, the women screamed and ran past a cedar rampart, cleverly disguised to hide men who waited with muskets aimed.

As expected, the enemy followed. At a signal, Squamish men fired all their guns simultaneously and kept shooting until the entire Euclataw force fell dead. The decoy was successful!

From that day on, Ki-ap-a-la-no was a hero and the champion of his people. He was a tall, powerful man with full hair and a resonant voice that was both gentle and commanding. His tolerance and good deeds won him a respect more significant than that commanded by his prowess as a fighter. With him always were the pacifism and spirituality that he absorbed in his youth from Luhk. He was a *sia'm* and, at Temlaham's death, he became Te Kiapalanoq.

During one Euclataw raid in Howe Sound, the Squamish had kidnapped a high-ranking Euclataw maiden. Now, to guarantee lasting peace, they arranged her marriage to Paytsauma, half-brother of Ki-ap-a-la-no. At a celebration lasting several months, the two peoples formed an enduring friendship. Until white men began to infiltrate the inlet, Indians there lived without fear of an aggressor.

In later years Ki-ap-a-la-no (then called Chief) often camped at Papiak, home of his son Lahwa. One day Ki-ap-a-la-no met John Morton, known as the first white settler on the inlet. When Morton told him that he had pre-empted vast acreage in that area, Ki-ap-a-la-no flinched, knowing that Indian sacred places lay there. Morton also admitted that he had invaded Deadman's Island, a sacred burial ground where natives had lashed burial boxes in trees surrounded by red fire-flowers, which, they believed, grew profusely from warriors' blood shed there.

"This land is not for whiteman potatoes," Ki-ap-a-la-no sadly told Morton.

CHAPTER XVIII

While settlers and missionaries crossed America, the "Fifty-four Forty or Fight" Polk presidential campaign threatened an Anglo-American war, demanding that the boundary be moved north to Russian Alaska on the 54th parallel. A treaty in 1846 ended years of bickering and established the international boundary at the 49th parallel. The new boundary ceded New Caledonia to the Hudson's Bay Company and the Columbia Department to the United States. Chief Factor James Douglas foresaw the terms of the treaty and in 1843 shifted Company headquarters from Fort Vancouver to the new Fort Victoria.

Upper and Lower Canada generally honoured a proclamation of George III a century before that prohibited anyone except the Crown from buying Indian land: *"Indians are to continue unmolested on their hunting grounds with titles intact until negotiated by treaty."*

In the West, however, officials decided that the edict did not apply to them! White settlers took whatever land they wanted. Vancouver Island became a colony in 1849 with Chief Factor Douglas as Royal Governor.

Douglas expressed concern for Indians. He felt that they were giving up their land willingly because they had no sense of its value. Hoping to purchase land titles, he applied for an Imperial loan; when it was denied, he planned to protect the Indians by laying out reserves around their villages. David, however, found reason to write to the new governor:

Dear Sir:
May I offer my congratulations on your becoming Governor of the new Vancouver Island Colony!
I speak as a close friend of the Musqueam people on the

Fraser River. We are grateful for your attempt to rectify land acquisition injustices. I respectfully call your attention to other injustices.

Inasmuch as you still are a Chief Factor of the Hudson's Bay Company, I shall direct to you my complaint that pertains both to the government and to the Company. Together, I understand, you recently divided the Indian people into "tribes," a term never used before. Your pretext was that language differences do not sufficiently distinguish natives. You fail to realize that Indians bond with kinship groups and do not need boundaries to separate them! And you now refer to the sia'ms *as "chiefs." Another new term you have introduced is the Chinook word "potlatch" for the native blanket-giving ceremony. These changes are extremely disturbing to the Indian people!*

I also am alarmed that white men are removing artifacts from the Northwest, taking them to museums or selling them as souvenirs! White scavengers even have appropriated some of our important archaeological middens!

Finally, I believe that white settlers should not preempt land from the Crown but should negotiate fairly with the Indians!

Respectfully yours, David Stewart.

2

David resumed his writing, compiling a record of intermingling of Indians and white men in the Pacific Northwest.

His personal experience and his total adherence to the Indian lifestyle lent exciting authenticity to his articles. Facing criticism, he often elaborated upon his growing conviction that white man's presence – and adoption of his habits by the Indians – was eroding native culture.

Sehla became pregnant, and David worried about the riskiness of childbirth for her. She contracted influenza during an epidemic in her final month of pregnancy, and she had a high fever when her labour began. Midwives attended her, David prayed, the shaman chanted, and Kukutwam implored his *siwcn*.

Sehla gave birth to a boy. David knelt and the women placed the infant between them. Then Sehla ceased to breathe. One woman took the baby and the other covered Sehla's face.

"Oh, please . . . help her," David begged. The midwives shook their heads.

With responsibility for care of his new son and the three older children, David had little time for grief. No one blamed him for the pregnancy; natives acknowledged no control over such things, and their concern centred on Kukutwam, whose death was expected to follow because he was Sehla's twin.

David raised his children in an extraordinary way. He encouraged their absorbing full Indian culture, but he taught them to read, write, and speak English until they were fluent in English, Halkomelem, and Chinook. For many years he instructed them in music, the classics, and the Bible. He tried to fill the void left by Sehla's death with love and education.

The children had both Indian and English names. Because they had a white father and grandfather, they were only one-fourth Indian, but Seth, the elder son, had full Indian characteristics. The two girls, Stella and Amanda, had dark hair but light complexions. Stella was married and widowed soon after the birth of a son, Hugh, who, like Seth, looked Indian. Louis, born at Sehla's death, had predominantly Caucasian features.

3

About 1850 David composed several articles for his publisher. The first described a general concern:

A decline in the aboriginal population is dismaying. The forts report diseases unknown to natives before white contact, such as measles, tuberculosis, and venereal disease. A siege of influenza has brought tragic loss to both Indians and white men. Infanticide is common, as white men father more half-breed babies. And alcohol takes its toll; the Company doesn't sell it, but it's available from the Americans!

The Company trades guns instead of rum – just as bad! After the Indians acquired guns, their intertribal raids turned into slaughter with enormous losses.

The Indians mimic our ways to their own destruction. For example, I'm told Simon Fraser's men "breathed fire in sticks with knobs on the end," introducing tobacco to Fraser River people. Now the Stalo make pipes and are so addicted they'll trade a night with one of their women for a bit of tobacco!

The second article contained observations about native religion:

Jesuit priests are on the Fraser River. Blackrobes, the Indians call them. One told me that he's an Oblate and that his order has set up missions in Victoria, preaching to Indians, British sailors, and Company families. Of course, the Company fosters Christianizing the Indians, but their men don't understand Indian nature. I hope the priests do.

Christianity is acceptable to Indians – it corresponds to their own beliefs. Native and Christian views of the world are similar. But in my opinion, Indians tend to adopt a sim-plified, rather materialistic version of Christianity that is not altogether sincere. Natives are ready converts because they're hungry for a stabilizing belief. At the same time, they want riches and often become opportunists.

4

After David dispatched the articles, he pondered returning to England. One day he called his family together.

"You are adults now," he began, "and I want you to have more education than I've been able to give you. In England – long my dream for you. Your dear mother would not have enjoyed going there, but I'd like to take you. Besides, you have cousins in England. Would . . . would you like to go?"

At first the young people were speechless. Then they squealed with excitement.

"My father," cried Seth, *"England?"*

"Yes, London! I have money saved from my writing, so you may stay as long as you like – at least while you study."

Seth spoke again. "My father, you have raised us as both Indian and English, but I'm different from Louis and my sisters because I *look* Indian."

"Does that matter?" asked David.

"No, I'm proud to be an Indian. To be a good Christian, I don't know. I go to mass at New Westminster and I listen to the blackrobes. Their message moves me but . . . confuses me, too."

"Why, Seth?"

"Because priests want us to give up Indian ways! Being Christian should not ask that! I want to study Christianity. To me, what the Oblates preach is not always what I think Jesus would say or what their God wants for us. Forgive me if I offend you."

David looked at Seth with wonder. "Forgive?" he

repeated. "There's nothing to forgive, son. I'm pleased that you raise questions. We think a lot alike. Yes, of course, you may study Christianity . . . Anglican, Roman Catholic – any denomination you choose."

Stella, Amanda, and Louis showered David with questions. "How long will it take to get there?" "When will we go?"

David hugged his daughters to him. "We'll go as soon as I can arrange passage! It will be a big change for you, my girls. There may be times when you'll long to be back in Mahli. And there's something I want all of you to remember."

"What is that?" asked Stella.

"Our people need help. The way of life they've known for generations has been changing. With education you may find ways to help them. Perhaps as Seth says, by examining the Christian message, perhaps in other ways. I may be too old, but you certainly are not!"

Seth leaped to his feet. "Too old? You are younger in spirit than any of us!"

David laughed. "I'll look into what accommodation is available. By the way, in the English culture you may address others by name directly. You girls would say 'Seth' rather than 'my brother,' for example, and call me 'father' instead of 'my father.' Also, as Indians you have used no surname, but abroad you'll be 'Stewarts'."

The Stewarts prepared for their voyage.

5

Before David left for England, Luhk said, "The governor wants river people to meet at Fort Langley. Please, will you go with me?"

"Now what the devil does he want?" David replied.

"Once I challenged Governor Simpson, and recently Governor Douglas. He may not be happy to see me. I'm angry!"

"Why are you angry?" asked Luhk.

"Mainly about changes. Yes, I'll go with you. Gladly!"

At the fort Governor Douglas stepped to the front of the room. "Welcome, my native friends," he began in Chinook. "And to you, sir," he added, looking at David.

David rose. "Thank you, sir," he said. "My name is David Stewart. You may recall a communication from me."

Douglas looked flustered and replied in an icy tone, "Ah, yes, I do indeed." He cleared his throat as if to regain composure and said, "I want all of you to know I'm still concerned about appropriation of Indian land, so I'm going ahead with my plan to create reserves."

"Where will they be?" David asked.

"Near white settlements where Indians can absorb culture. My idea was to offer you Indians as much land as you wanted."

"That's changed?" David did not conceal his annoyance.

"Yes, the Colonial Secretary has ruled that Indians have no right to any land beyond actual needs. I've called this meeting so you can see the boundaries." Douglas unrolled a map and hung it from a hook.

The Indians crowded around, and Luhk leaned forward. David leaped to his feet again, examined the map, and exclaimed, "The reserves are much too small!"

Breathing hard, Governor Douglas answered haughtily, "The surveyors allotted ten acres per man, but Indians may add any land they've cleared or tilled."

"Cleared or tilled!" David shouted. "These people are not farmers! They haven't cleared beyond their villages and they've tilled little land if any. They have no idea what they may need!"

"The Secretary ruled . . ."

David interrupted. "But the reserve plan is *yours!* I do believe you're sincere, sir, but I urge you to reconsider. I differ with what you call 'civilizing' the Indians!" There was a general murmur of agreement from Indians in the room.

Governor Douglas rose, impatient and obviously infuriated by David's arguments. "Enough!" he said loudly. "I've done all I can for you natives over the years. I've even tried to improve your spiritual standards. The reserve system is the best protection I can offer!" To terminate the discussion he gathered his papers and abruptly left the room.

"He's stubborn," said David sadly, as he and Luhk rowed home. "They call him 'Old Squaretoes.'"

6

David disliked leaving Luhk, with whom he had shared respect and understanding for many years. When they parted, Luhk placed his wrinkled hands on David's. "My friend," he said, "Indian legend says spirits of good people fly south with the wild geese. Your Sehla flies with them and comes back at moons of spring. You will come back, too."

"I will, Luhk. Yes, I will." David vowed. He also vowed to put aside his dismay and enjoy the trip with his family.

CHAPTER XIX

Not long after David's departure, Luhk longed for his advice. When Indians thronged to the river in 1858 for summer fishing, they found a jumble of tents and shacks at their inherited sites. White men were panning gravel bars in Indian fishing grounds! Indians could not set up their weirs and nets. White men had discovered gold!

A miner had found some gold on the upper Fraser, and some Californians discovered a rich yield at Hill's Bar. Pandemonium erupted! More than thirty thousand prospectors, mostly American, went to Fort Langley. Rafts and boats jammed the river; oxen, mules, and horses trampled the banks.

Traders, merchants, and saloon-keepers arrived with the prospectors, transforming Victoria and Fort Langley into boom towns. Soon Victoria resembled San Francisco with gaslights, fire-wagons, four-story buildings, high-priced land – and prostitutes. Fort Langley was chaotic.

Frustrated by losing their fishing spots, a few Indians became guides. Some, including Kwahl, panned for gold themselves, learning to swirl sand and gravel in a pan with the hope of finding gold flakes. Most, however, discovered the value of gold and resented the strangers who were taking it from them. In a general uprising they pulled up miners' claim stakes and pilfered their supplies; bodies of miners often floated downriver.

In the heat of the turmoil, Governor Douglas acted on his fear that the inundation of Americans would result in United States claims on the Fraser. On November 19, 1858 he established the Crown Colony of British Columbia on the mainland and declared English law to be in effect there. He revoked the Hudson's Bay Company's fur-trade empire and fishing monopoly on the Fraser

River, but this had no effect on the friction between miners and Indians. Douglas urgently begged military protection! The Colonial Secretary replied:

"Our goal is to secure the entire river valley for civilized man through agriculture. I'm dispatching a hand-picked corps of 165 Royal Engineers to police the gold rush and open up more land for settlement."

The Royal Engineers included masons, printers, painters, draftsmen, surveyors, architects, carpenters, blacksmiths, and sappers – soldiers who built fortifications.

"We'll clear land for barracks and call the place Sapperton," Colonel Moody, the commander, directed. "Langley is inadequate for defence against American forces, so we'll move the mainland capital from there to the north riverbank and name it Queensborough."

The engineers felled trees, dug stumps, and battled mud and mosquitoes. By June 1859 parks and avenues took shape with a saloon, churches, and a general store; lots sold at a two hundred-dollar average. The new town, renamed New Westminster, was the port of entry for the mainland colony, with unsettled English Bay as an alternate anchorage.

The Royal Engineers constructed a four-hundred-mile road – the Cariboo Wagon Road – from Hope to Barkerville after "nuggets by the ton" attracted thousands of miners to the Interior. Barkerville became the largest city north of San Francisco; it bore the name of Billy Barker, a Cornish seaman who found a vein of gold that netted him $600,000.

2

More Oblate clergy came to Mahli soon after the Royal Engineers arrived at the river. On a raw December day, Father Leon Fouquet stepped ashore from a canoe. Maintaining his vows of poverty, chastity, and obedience, he proclaimed that he wished "to preach the gospel to the poor."

Father Fouquet wore a belted cassock with a gold crucifix hanging from his neck. He raised his wide-brimmed hat and made the sign of a cross, which the Indians interpreted as a peace symbol. Trying to win confidence with friendship, he shook hands with Luhk and the villagers and led a long prayer session. He taught as much of the catechism as he could manage in Chinook and tried to explain that the church banned drinking, murders motivated by revenge, herbal birth control, and – above all – polygamy. He ordered men to abandon all wives but one and concubines to give up prostitution. After offering confession, he baptized and served Holy Communion to those persons whom he considered worthy.

After Kah-te's death Luhk no longer was guilty of polygamy. But he was aware that the clergy did not understand Indians and looked on them as heathens. He was sad as he received the mass, and he did not look forward to his enforced move to the Musqueam Reserve. He recalled words David had written before his departure:

The trapper, the settler, and the missionary scoff at Indian tradition and cultural values. The government and the Hudson's Bay Company want to transform Indians into Englishmen, and missionaries want to claim them as Christians. I hope for the protection of my Indian friends!

CHAPTER XX

The Stewarts sailed to Victoria on the Hudson's Bay Company steamer *Otter*. There they took rooms while David outfitted the boys with shirts and trousers and bought dresses and petticoats for Stella and Amanda. Wearing shoes for the first time, the young people hobbled after David and found the new garments scratchy and restraining. By sailing day, however, they pranced about in their finery and boarded the steamer with enthusiasm. In Panama they stayed in dingy rooms to await the weekly train across the isthmus. Heat sapped their energy, ruffians on the streets made walking unsafe, mosquitoes buzzed constantly, and the smell of inadequate plumbing sickened them.

David chuckled at the distress of his children. "You'd rather be at Mahli, wouldn't you, my dears? Never mind, we'll pass the time with some lessons in etiquette and table manners."

When the family reached London, an autumnal evening fog cloaked the city; gas lights glistened in a yellowish haze and bells pealed into the night. David rented a flat, showed the sights, and took his family to tailors, cobblers, and haberdashers. Then he contacted his brother Ian, whom he had not seen for almost thirty years.

Ian had adult children. At first, conversation between the two families was stiff, but it gradually became spirited. On Ian's recommendations David selected schools, and within a month he and his family had settled into a comfortable flat in Kensington. Quickly, David's family adopted the proper English of their cousins and abandoned Chinook and their Indian adaptation of English. Louis enrolled in university classes, Amanda found an active social life, and Stella devoted her time to little Hugh, seven then and sickly, and to her father. David contacted his publisher for a new assignment.

Seth investigated religious study. "I like the Anglican Church," he said, "but Catholicism appeals to me more. I'd like to enter a seminary."

"And be ordained?"

"I'm not sure. I want to find out why religion stirs up our people at home and demands so much change for them. Our people need a belief in Jesus and a loving God, but they need protection, too – from those in the church who don't understand us. Like you, Father, I want to help, but first I must find some answers!"

David put his arms about Seth. "My son, you have my blessing. You know that I challenge what the government and the missionaries are doing to the Indians! Do as you see fit and know I'll stand by you."

The Stewart young people had trouble adapting to the prim modesty and pompousness of the Victorian era. Their naïvete subjected them to unpleasantness. As David feared, they met snobbish rebuffs because of their mixed blood. Among themselves they confessed a dislike of English food; of London's smoke, soot, and murky fog; of the damp chill of most buildings; and of the sight of many people reduced to begging. They contracted colds and worried about effect of the environment on Hugh. But they withheld their feelings from David.

2

At first, Hugh enjoyed becoming an English schoolboy, but he soon perceived that other boys made fun of him. "They don't like me because I'm Indian," he told Stella. He spent most leisure hours alone, and he often had wheezing attacks.

Watching Hugh choke back tears when she asked him about his classes, Stella decided to visit the school. Before she went, however, the school headmaster called on her. She knew instinctively that he bore bad news.

"Please don't be alarmed, Mrs. Stewart. Hugh has been in a scuffle, but he's all right," the headmaster said.

Stella paled. "Wh . . . where is he?"

"We took him to the hospital. It's three streets from here, but I've a buggy. Come, I'll drive you there."

Stella trembled with fright as she reached for her cape and hurried to the rig. "Tell me," she beseeched.

"It's his leg . . . it may be broken. Boys can be rough without knowing . . .."

Without knowing? I wonder, thought Stella.

"Mrs. Stewart," said the headmaster when they reached the hospital, "please excuse me. I must get back, but I'll return after classes."

Stella darted into the building, A roly-poly aide led her to a waiting room and told her that Hugh was in surgery. "The physician will come to speak to you. Cheer up, dearie," she said. "Boys must break a bone now and then, y'know!"

Alone in the room, Stella found no cheer. A shaft of sunlight beamed through a window high on the wall and blinded her slightly. She stared at hundreds of tiny dust particles that danced up and down on the rays, her anxiety seeming to mingle with them. She did not see the door open, and she jumped nervously at the sound of a voice.

"You . . . you're Hugh's mother? Oh, I startled you! I'm the doctor caring for your son." A man stepped from the shadowy side of the room into the sunlight and smiled at her, extending his hand. Appearing to be about thirty, he had a hard-muscled build; his brow and dark side-whiskers were full. A stethoscope dangled from his neck over a white smock. He was not handsome, but to Stella he had the most engaging smile she ever had seen.

"Y . . . yes," Stella stammered, grasping the doctor's hand mechanically. "My son, how . . . how is he?"

"Please," said the doctor, "sit here where we can talk." He motioned to a bench. "I don't want you to worry, Mrs. Stewart. His leg was broken in two places, and nasty cracks they were, but they should mend nicely. Quite a spill he must have had."

"I . . . I'm not sure it was a spill. The other boys . . ." The doctor's face softened with understanding. "I can guess," he said. "It's because he's Indian?"

Stella fought an impulse to unburden her distress to this man whom she barely knew. "Yes," she replied. "There's been trouble. And you must have noticed how delicate he is."

"I did. We watched his breathing in the surgery, but we can treat that, too, as his leg heals." Sitting there in the sunlight, the doctor stared at Stella, thinking her enchantingly lovely and wondering at her being the mother of the Indian boy. He knew that questioning her would be too forward, but he had an odd feeling that his asking would not offend her. "Come, we'll go to your son. He should be coming out of anaesthesia. By the way, my name is Peter Lee." Holding the door for Stella at the ward, he smiled at her again, his eyes clear and steady.

As he wakened, Hugh whimpered with pain. Stella prepared to spend the night at the hospital.

The headmaster appeared briefly, excusing himself as soon as possible with a promise to punish the boys who caused the injury. Stella sensed his relief at finding Hugh in a satisfactory condition and his obligation at an end.

Peter Lee remained at the hospital until late in the evening and did not conceal his attraction to Stella. He brought supper and tea to her while Hugh slept.

"I'm not imposing on your time?" asked Stella, striving to hide the excitement she felt in his presence.

"Certainly not! Mrs. Stewart, at the risk of being presumptuous, I'd like you to call me Peter."

"Yes, Peter, I'd like that. I'm Stella." She laughed with pleasure. "To me that's not presumptuous at all. I'll tell you right now I'm not a proper English lady. Perhaps you'd be shocked to know I never wore shoes until I came here this year. Also, I'm Indian like my son except that my white blood shows more. And I like being Indian!"

Peter threw back his head in mirth. "Bravo, Stella! And since you are candid, may I ask about . . . well, your husband?"

"I'm a widow. My white father brought my family here to educate us."

Peter's face was alive with interest, but he said seriously, "I'm concerned about Hugh's apparent bronchitis, which may be harder to treat than his leg – if you want me to, that is."

"Yes, yes! I've been intending to seek treatment for him."

"We'll try something new from the chemist. But you must tell me the other problem, Stella. I'll be caring for him for some time and maybe I can help."

"Well, he's an unhappy child. You were right – it's because he's Indian. The other boys are unkind, and I guess he tried to fight back today, scrawny as he is." Stella's eyes were teary.

Peter wanted to comfort Stella, to put his arms about her and protect her from hurt. Gently he patted the back of her hand. "Children can be cruel," he said kindly. "If only they could understand that all of us are the same under our skins! Rest assured, I'll do what I can." He smiled at Stella and shook her hand. Then he secured a cot for her and departed for the night.

"They called me a half-breed and I tried to fight 'cause I know that's a bad name," Hugh sobbed the next day, when Stella and Peter asked him about the accident. "Why?"

Stella hugged her child against her and saw Peter's face fill with compassion. When she started home to change her clothing, he asked, "May I walk with you?" Before they reached her flat, he turned to her. "I'm going to be bold once more. I'd like to see you again, other than at the hospital."

Stella's cheeks flushed with pleasure. "I . . . I'd like that, too, Peter."

Peter laughed. "It's refreshing to find a woman so honest and . . . unstuffy! You know, of course, a correct English lady would coyly blush at such an invitation!"

They both laughed.

3

In a few days Hugh was home, resting in a cast, and Peter called frequently. When he came to the flat, Stella gaped in admiration, for he had replaced the white hospital smock with a velvet-lapelled tailcoat and matching vest, plaid trousers, black silk cravat, and top hat.

After Peter examined Hugh in the early evenings, he and Stella left Amanda or David in charge and went walking. They chatted with animation and often went to dinner, a concert, or the theatre. On mild Sundays they strolled in Hyde Park and stopped for tea.

Peter was five years older than Stella. He wanted to share ideals and discuss beliefs. "I've never married," he said. "My mother sacrificed for my education, so I cared for her until she died earlier this year. I've engaged in tutoring to increase my income, so I could help Hugh with his school work."

David, Seth, and Louis liked Peter, and Amanda considered Stella fortunate. They welcomed his frequent visits.

"Medicine was not my chosen profession," Peter told Stella. "It was to please my mother. The great desire of my youth, believe it or not, was to travel to your part of the world! I've read the Cook and Vancouver journals and studied the history and geography. And Indian beliefs intrigue me. You and I were destined to meet, Stella!"

"Yes," replied Stella, her voice low.

Peter celebrated Christmas with the Stewarts, and the bleak winter wore on.

Hugh did not respond to treatment. "He could go back to school on crutches except for his health and the hazard of icy sidewalks," Peter said. "Frankly, he's better off staying out of the fog until we can control his wheezing. He has asthmatic bronchitis, and I suspect a spot on his lungs."

One night Stella sat by Hugh's side as he tossed restlessly and coughed so violently that she feared he would not recover. She was distraught. The next evening, while Hugh napped, she lit the parlour candles and sat with Peter on the chesterfield. They stared listlessly into coals glowing in the grate.

"We've done all we can, Stella. Admitting Hugh to the hospital would be no help. I see only one solution," Peter said. "He needs to breathe clean air. He must get out of London!"

"But . . . but where?" Stella asked. Then she blurted, "Oh, Peter, do you know where I want to take him? Home, back where we came from! I don't like England! If only it didn't mean leaving you! I . . . I don't want to leave you!" She sobbed.

Peter pressed Stella's hand. "You *should* go home! But I won't let you leave me! I'll go with you!"

"You . . . you'd go with me?"

Peter drew Stella to him. "My darling, I'm in love with you! It's too early for me to tell you, I know, but I want to marry you, to take care of you and dear Hugh. I'll be a good father – I love him, too! Stella, is it too soon? Will you marry me?"

Rapturously, Stella said, "I've loved you from that first afternoon at the hospital when sunbeams danced around us and you smiled at me. Yes, oh, yes, Peter!"

Stella went limp with want when Peter leaned across the settee and his lips met hers. His hand brushed a breast and closed over it, and she felt his passion. Shaken, they held each other tightly, then drew apart, knowing they must curb desire while they were in the parlour. They needed to talk.

"London is not special to me," Peter said, fingers locked in Stella's. "My mother was my only family, so I can close my office without a qualm. I've inherited a comfortable sum, too. Yes, I'll go home with you and set up practice there! Do you think I can compete with your medicine-men? After all, they've satisfied your people for centuries!"

"I know you can!"

"Stella, you've told me of smallpox, influenza, and other diseases there. Medical science can treat those! And if your Musqueams on the river don't need me, there's Burrard Inlet. I've found it on the map and read that logging and white settlement have taken hold there. Maybe Burrard Inlet would welcome a doctor, one with a wife and son! How does that strike you?"

"Yes, yes! I can't believe how lucky I am," Stella replied, shaken by Peter's ardour and his sensational plan. "To have you and for Hugh to be well, too! But it'll be hard to leave my father, Peter. He's withdrawn and he needs me, because my brothers are off studying and Amanda is usually with beaux."

David depended on Stella's companionship. As a published authority on the history of the Pacific Northwest, he was in demand as a lecturer. But he was lonely. He admitted to himself that he was more comfortable with Luhk and his native friends than with his brother and his countrymen. He could not speak freely and he antagonized most Englishmen with his defence of Indian rights. Writing was difficult; his pen flowed more freely in his adopted country among the cedars and ancient traditions. He did not speak of his unhappiness as he watched his children react to the new world unfolding before them, but he suspected that all of them would like to go home. He rejoiced for Stella.

"I approve of your decision to go back, my Stella," David told her wistfully. "Incidentally, Peter," he added, "you mentioned settling at Burrard Inlet. Well, Governor Douglas has offered 160 acres to any British subject who pre-empts there. You'd do well to take advantage of that!"

Within a week Peter sold his practice, secured passage reservations, and married Stella in a simple family service. Eager to move Hugh from London rapidly, Peter and Stella bought medical supplies – enough, Stella teased, to open an apothecary of their own – packed their belongings and Peter's books, bundled Hugh warmly, and departed. Stella's happiness overpowered the heartache she felt in leaving David and her family.

PART IV

The Muddle

CHAPTER XXI

The Royal Engineers forbade slavery, which ended intertribal wars and raiding for slaves. Indians from the North found an alternative: a summer pilgrimage to Victoria to camp around the fort and carouse on the beaches. But that activity became a debauch. Many Indians made a business of prostitution, renting their women and girls for whiskey or Hudson's Bay Company blankets. They went home with blankets and liquor, but they also took alcohol addiction and syphilitic ulcers.

Afraid of inciting war, the government refrained from using its gunboats. Then calamity struck – the most devastating smallpox epidemic ever experienced, which between 1862 and 1864 killed one-third of the native population of the two colonies!

While Oblate priests tended the sick and supervised vaccinations in Victoria, the Indians spread smallpox northward in their retreat. The *Colonist* reported that Victoria woodlands were *"white with blanched bones of the victims."* Unable to cope with the death toll, government workers let corpses rot or piled them in mounds and covered them with branches.

Stella, Peter, and Hugh docked in Victoria during the height of the chaos. They had no fear of the disease, because Peter had vaccinated them, but they looked at the corpses with horror.

"Stay away from Burrard Inlet," a government clerk advised. "The Squamish are on the warpath."

"Why?" Peter asked.

"Well, Indians didn't mind the first settlers in the inlet, but when they realized whiteman started the pox, they got mean. 'Too many whiteman!' they say."

"Will the military step in?"

"The Engineers threaten to wipe out the whole tribe! As I said, stay away from there!"

"We're headed for New Westminster, so I can register and see about a pre-empt. We should be safe there."

On the way upriver aboard the *Otter* Stella pointed to familiar spots and flung out her arms. "Isn't it glorious, Peter?" she cried. "Just smell the pure air! The first thing I want to do is visit Mahli!"

Hugh had begun to improve. He limped slightly, but his cough had disappeared. On the day Peter hired a rower to take them to Mahli, Hugh shared his mother's excitement.

Stella was aghast to find Mahli almost deserted and its buildings in shambles. Smallpox had reduced the population so drastically that survivors had moved to the Musqueam Reserve.

"Here's our old home," Stella cried, as she walked about and paused at a broken-down house. A post carved with Luhk's crest lay crazily askew, and a rat scampered across the sill. "Gone! In such a short time! My relatives must be at the reserve!"

"Then let's go there," said Peter.

At the reserve Stella found a cousin, Kukutwam's son. "I was sad when your father died," she said. She explained to Peter the belief that one twin must follow the other in death. "The thunderbird struck with lightning."

"Yes, I remember. And Luhk?"

"Luhk is gone, too. And his wife, old granny Tahulet."

Stella bowed her head. She shared her father's admiration of Luhk. "So Luhk's son Kwahl is *sia'm?*" she asked.

"In secret. We have a chief now, and the priests do for us."

Aware that her cousin eyed Peter nervously and stared at her bonnet, gown, and leather shoes almost with distrust, Stella realized that her people would consider her a stranger. She felt a pang of hurt but found Kwahl and introduced him to Peter.

"Ah, Kwa-sehla!" Kwahl greeted Stella, using her Indian name and speaking in Chinook. "Welcome. You'll find changes if you come here! Whiteman law – Indian Act – says you're not Indian. If Indian woman marries a whiteman, she loses what whiteman calls status. You don't own any reserve property and you can't be buried here. Same for your child. Not for a man though. If a man marries a white woman, he gives her status."

"That's not fair!" cried Stella.

"No. Whiteman law is not good. They took my sons, too. Sent them to a mission school. Blackrobes say they teach our children a better way to live. We'll see. Too many Musqueam are unhappy and drink too much. Sometimes my sons are drunk."

Stella grasped Kwahl's hand in pity. Sadly, she recognized not only the end of ties with her people but with the uncomplicated way of life she had known with them. "I'd rather live at Burrard Inlet even if the Squamish are making trouble there," she said later to Peter. "My life here died with Mahli. Just as Father predicted."

Peter obtained a pre-empt. "It's part of a townsite on the inlet south shore," he said. "The Royal Engineers are clearing there on government orders and have stopped the Squamish uprising. They're protecting the inlet against American invasion, too, I'm told, with military reserves. But I want to inspect conditions myself."

2

Peter and Stella enrolled Hugh in classes in New Westminster and hired a lady to look after him for several days. Then they took seats in a horse-drawn coach that traversed the new North Road to Burrard Inlet.

"A bit bumpy," laughed Stella as the carriage jolted over ruts and passengers lurched from side to side.

"Yes," replied Peter, "but it's like being in a green tunnel! Just see those trees, hundreds of feet high!"

The carriage emerged at the terminal, where several steamers were at anchor; wild geese pecked along the mud flats, and sawbill ducks glided in the shallows.

"This is where I want to live, Stella!" Peter cried.

A dock worker told them that inlet activity was on the north shore. "Man named Graham started a mill there," he said. "Navvy Jack Thomas will ferry you across. Mind you watch for drunk Indians!"

"I thought the Indian trouble was over," Peter replied.

"Indians will always be trouble!"

Stella cringed at the bigoted viewpoint, but Peter advised her not to protest.

"The village is straight ahead," explained Navvy Jack, as he rowed them to the north shore, "and Graham's Pioneer Mill a bit to the east, where smoke is coming through the trees."

Firs, cedars, and hemlocks dwarfed the tiny settlement at the base of Grouse Mountain; farms dotted the edges of the town. At the wharf, swarthy longshoremen shouted as they loaded planks into the hold of a stern wheeler.

From the dock Stella and Peter followed a boardwalk to a cluster of shacks. Gingerly they stepped over puddles matted with sawdust. A blacksmith waved from a forge, and an aroma of fresh bread drifted from a bakery. A few Indians loitered on the walk.

Graham greeted them. "Only Indians here when I came," he said. "Then a few engineers took their grants here. Take a look at that reservoir above my works. A sapper at Lynn Creek lets me flume some of his water. I drive two wheels and a planing machine. The second flume brings down the shingle-bolts."

"You're shipping lumber?" Peter asked.

"Regularly!" Graham paused and eyed Peter's London attire and unblemished hands. "You want to join us, do you?"

"Well," replied Peter, "I've put in for land across the water, but there's nothing there yet, so this would be a better spot for us. I'm a doctor."

"A doctor! We'd like to have you, though I can't promise many patients 'til we grow! But I was a builder – I could put up a house for you . . ."

"Thank you. We'll seriously consider coming here."

"Good. Now, before you go, notice those spars in the water. From trees with nary a branch below sixty feet. Perfect!"

Shaking hands, Peter said, "Prospects do look good for your mill, Mr. Graham. There's just one thing. I'm concerned about the Indians here. Are they as boisterous as we've heard?"

"They're boisterous all right – the bloody whiskey's doing it! Squamish are moving down from Howe Sound in droves, and whites are coming here, too, but the government's in control. It's safe."

"What do we have to think about?" asked Stella. "If you want to settle here, Peter, so do I!"

"All right, then! At least 'til the south shore develops!" Peter replied enthusiastically.

Graham agreed to have a house ready for them in a week.

3

Peter and Stella shopped for furnishings, tubs, and a wood cooking stove. By paddle-wheel steamer they transported their purchases with their trunks and medical supplies. Millhands, white and Indian, helped them carry possessions into their new log home, which was crude but chinked to be airtight. They placed the tubs and stove in one corner and lined up beds behind a curtain. One worker rigged a drainboard; others dug a well, put up an outhouse, and stacked wood.

When the workers refused pay, Peter promised them free medical attention. He had picked up Chinook quickly on his own, and he made a point of using it as much as he could. He shook hands with several Indians who had been drinking. Maybe I can help them, he thought, if I can get to know them. Before the workers left, he went into a small anteroom built as his office. Smiling at his new friends, he dusted off the shingle he had brought from England and tacked it on the door.

4

Peter's patients were few at first, but before long mill and dock workers appeared at his door with fever, lacerations, and varied complaints. Most were white, because Indians were slow to relinquish faith in their medicinemen. One day, however, an Indian came, carrying another who was drunk and bleeding profusely from a mangled foot.

"He's Billy Jimmy," the Indian said. "Accident."

One look convinced Peter that he could not save the foot, and he prepared for amputation, loath as he was to undertake surgery without medical facilities. He sterilized

equipment in boiling water and sedated Billy with lau-
danum and a whiff of ether. With the other Indian holding Billy's shoulders, Peter completed the amputation,
stemmed the blood flow, and bandaged the stump. He prepared a cot and kept Billy with him.

The wound healed without infection, and within a
week Billy hobbled about on makeshift crutches. Only
later did Peter visualize what his reputation would have
become, had Billy died. As it was, Billy became a friend
and influenced other Indians to trust Peter.

"My grandsire, Atsaian, was a Squamish *sia'm*," Billy
told Peter and Stella. My father was a chief, too. Whiteman
didn't like his name. Changed it to Jimmy."

"So," said Stella. "They called you Billy, and you use
your father's name as surname. Billy Jimmy, right?" When
Billy nodded, she exclaimed, "You're a *sia'm*, too! You're
Chief Jimmy!"

"All right, then, Chief Billy Jimmy," said Peter, "I'm
going to help you give up alcohol. It's bad for you."

"Maybe little bit?"

"I can't allow that, Billy. You don't want more accidents
like this one, which cost you a foot!" Peter sighed with distress that alcoholism was a problem not just for Billy but
for most Indians at Pioneer Mill.

Several months later, Billy hobbled into Peter's office
with a cane and no crutches.

"You have a new foot!" exclaimed Peter.

Billy pulled up his legging to display an artificial foot
ingeniously held to his leg with cedar withes.

"You . . . you made this yourself?"

Billy smiled. From a knapsack he took a cedar carving,
polished to perfection. "For you," he said shyly.

"I'm overwhelmed. It's superb!" Peter said. "Stella,
come see this!"

"These symbols, Peter," Stella said, "are the sun, raven, eagle, beaver, and the bear mother. This one with the beak and big talons is the thunderbird, and there's a story to how you've arranged them. Right, Billy?"

Grinning, Billy said, "I . . . I don't drink now."

"I'm proud of you!" Peter said warmly. "Now you can be a good chief for your people. Chief Billy Jimmy!"

The Indians adopted Peter as an equal after he treated Billy. They took Peter and Hugh fishing and hunting and often brought gifts to the door: a salmon, firewood, a basket of salmonberries, or a bow and sheaf of arrows for Hugh.

5

In England Stella had speedily discarded Indian customs; now a return to native housekeeping did not tempt her. To her a bed was more comfortable than a grass mat, a stove was superior to a fire pit, and the convenience of tinned salmon surpassed drying salmon on racks in the rafters. But she worked hard.

"Too much drudgery for you," fretted Peter.

"No, we're building a new life here. And I have you and Hugh, all I want!"

The first winter the Lees spent at Pioneer Mill was unusually cold for the normally mild Pacific Northwest. Snow fell atop the mountains for months and frequently covered the lowlands. A dense fog hung low on the water night after night.

"Almost like London," Peter remarked.

"Except this is clean fog, and it's not bothering Hugh," Stella replied. "We need to be here."

6

Deeply concerned about alcoholism, Squamish Chief Snat often discussed the situation with Peter. He wanted to save his people.

"Perhaps the Oblate priest can help when he comes on his next circuit," suggested Peter.

"Father Fouquet is kind. I'll ask him!"

Chief Snat begged Father Fouquet to mediate with the military authorities about controlling alcoholism. In exchange, he agreed to convert as many Squamish people as he could to Catholicism.

"I'll start a mission on the north shore," agreed Father Fouquet. "You find a place."

Chief Snat chose Ustlaun, a mile west of the mill. The village was picturesque each spring when a grove of wild cherry trees burst into blossom. The Oblates named Father Fouquet supervisor of the mission and constructed a chapel, which became Our Lady of Seven Sorrows Church. The government laid out Mission Reserve at the chapel site – thirty-five acres with an eighteen hundred-foot waterfront. Squamish wishing to become Catholic occupied white cottages among the cherry trees.

Because of his fearlessness and genuine love for Indians, Father Fouquet managed to bring order to the Squamish. He had to offer a faith as potent as the desire for alcohol.

7

"Men at the mill think they need more than Father Fouquet," Peter told Stella. "They've taken Colonial advice and formed a militia unit. Personally, I can't see the need.

I have no quarrel with Indians." He stretched in his chair, enjoying free time.

Stella laughed. "No, the Indians here are your friends. They know you care about them. And your Indian wife and son will protect you." She laughed again and said, "But your son is with his friends and I'm an Indian who *does* attack – like this!" She bolted the door, drew the curtain, and pulled Peter to the bed.

Peter slipped the pins from her hair and ran his hands through its fullness. As he made love to her, Stella was uninhibited. "I'm glad I married a primitive woman," Peter said.

8

Thomas Graham failed financially and had to sell Pioneer Mill. His successor operated the business until he, too, went bankrupt. When a third owner, Sewell Prescott Moody, took over the mill, he prospered, and the village became known as Moodyville.

"Just call me Sue," Moody said. "I'm an American and not related to the Engineers' Colonel Moody!" A likeable man, Moody also was resolute. He expanded from milling local logs to processing great booms from the North.

The Moody Mill began to ship to world markets, and two other major mills flourished on the inlet's south shore. One was Stamp's Mill, which Captain Edward Stamp opened next to the townsite laid out by the Royal Engineers. The other belonged to Jeremiah Rogers, who called his clearing Jericho. Burrard Inlet was astir!

CHAPTER XXII

Little by little, Father Fouquet and the Oblates replaced the Squamish class system with white men's values. Many natives seemed to become white in spirit. Preaching at Mission Reserve, Bishop Paul Durieu announced his "system": prohibition of dancing, drinking, gambling, shamanism, and potlatching, all of which he called heathenism. "Do not trust the *sia'm*, shaman, or medicine-man," he commanded. "They are charlatans who hypnotize for evil purposes. Priests are your leaders."

Some Indians gathered in Peter's office to protest the regulations. Billy said, "The blackrobes teach love, but whiteman doesn't love the Indian." He shook his head.

"I promised to make Squamish into Catholics. I'm not sure now," added Chief Snat.

Billy waved his arms. "We watched whiteman dig up land where greens and berries grew to plant wheat and corn that he has to take care of!"

"And we have to use whiteman names!" cried Chief Snat.

Peter said, "Maybe so he can spell them."

"No need."

Some Squamish at Mission Reserve rebelled and moved to Moodyville, and some went to the Capilano Reserve at Homulchesen, which did not enforce Catholicism. Another group, *Tsleil-waututh* (People of the Inlet), occupied their hunting grounds at Second Narrows. However, disease, alcoholism, and declining morals had so weakened most of the Squamish at Mission Reserve that they clung to the security of the reserve. Women hid their elongated heads under long hair, and men vied for hats and white men's hand-me-downs. They hoped that white ways would be superior to their own; they put trust in white leadership. Even Chief Snat buried his doubts and defended the Durieu system; and Billy Jimmy said he was glad to have the church take care of him.

2

On May 24, 1864, Moodyville celebrated Queen Victoria's birthday with fireworks and canoe races. Chief Snat asked Sue Moody to read a letter to the new governor, Frederick Seymour, signed by most of the local chiefs, Squamish and Musqueam:

Great Chief English:
We beg to speak to you. We, the native Indians, gather to show you our good dispositions.

We know the good heart of the Queen for the Indians. You bring that good heart with you, so we are happy to welcome you.

We wish to become good Indians and to be friends with white people.

Please to protect us against any bad Indians or bad white men. Please to protect our land, that it will not be small, for us; many are pleased with their reservations, and many wish that reservations be marked out for them.

Please to give good things to make us become like the good white men, as exchange for our land occupied by white men. Our heart will always be good and thankful to the Queen, and to you, Great Chief.

We finish to speak to you.

Stella wiped a tear as she listened to the words. "I don't know whether to cry or scream 'hogwash!'" she said. "Whiteman has killed Indian spirit!"

3

Months passed between letters from David, so Stella did not know that Amanda had sailed for British Columbia until she arrived on the arm of a gentleman.

"Amanda!" cried Stella, hugging her sister. "What a surprise!"

"Father didn't tell you? Maybe it was the slow post. Anyway, Stella, this is my husband, Angus McMechen."

Hearing Stella and Amanda, Peter and Hugh rushed in.

"Sit down and tell us everything!" demanded Stella, unfastening her apron. "It's so wonderful to see you!"

Amanda glanced at Angus and said, "I wanted to come sooner but hated to ask Father for passage money. Then I heard about the London Emigration Society. It paid my fare."

"What's the London Emigration Society?"

"It brings girls to Victoria to find employment – more to supply wives for all the single men, I think. Then on the ship I met Angus. He was returning to Victoria from a business trip."

"Aye, I'm a commission merchant," said Angus. He chuckled. "I took one look at this bonnie lass and decided I'd not let some greedy mon snatch her away. Praises be, an Anglican priest was aboard who married us on the high seas!"

Amanda smiled demurely. "Oh, Stella, Victoria is wonderful!" she said. "Fancy balls and theatre . . . so much! Why don't you . . . do you really like living here in this . . ." Embarrassed, she broke off her words.

Stella observed Amanda's hoop-skirted gown, hair coiled into ringlets, and brooch sparkling on a lace bertha. She laughed. Patting her abdomen, she replied, "We like it here! Balls aren't for us. And you can see we've started a family."

Peter put an arm about Stella. "Maybe I should wonder how she'll raise this baby," he teased. "She's happiest in a Squamish tunic with bare legs and hair hanging loose."

"They don't think of me as Indian in Victoria," Amanda went on. "I don't look it. Besides, it's not important. Half-breed isn't an insult there. Why, I heard that Governor Douglas has two daughters who've had their heads flattened!"

They all laughed. Then Stella said, "Tell us about Father."

"He lectures and writes some," Amanda replied. "He misses this country but wants to stay in London until Louis earns his degree. There's a lady, but he hasn't mentioned marriage."

"And Seth? What about him?"

"You don't know? Seth's here on the coast! He never was ordained, but he's with a Roman Catholic order, teaching at a mission school farther north. The priests don't seem to mind that he looks Indian. I'm sure he'll come to see you."

4

Seth's assignment was a residential school north of Howe Sound. On the voyage from England with some missionaries, he discovered with dismay that they made no attempt to understand Indian ways. He felt even more dismay when he arrived at the settlement and examined the residential school.

The school consisted of a classroom, kitchen, residences for priests and nuns, and separate dormitories for boys and girls. The children were from distant villages, usually brought forcibly to the school by the church. Isolated and alienated from their families, they remained for at least ten months of each year.

A stern priest and a nun greeted the children on arrival, stripped and sprayed them with disinfectant, and assigned non-native names to them. Then the priest said, "Speak English only or you get the strap."

After mandatory daily mass, the priests forced the children to perform manual labour: digging the garden, feeding stock, and performing household chores. They banned all indigenous customs and replaced them with their own morals and methods.

"The children are not learning to read," Seth said to the priests. "All you teach is catechism."

"The ungrateful heathens aren't worth the trouble," one priest replied.

"Stupid savages, that's what they are!" added another.

"I resent that!" Seth flared. "Education to you is no more than converting children to Catholicism!"

"Watch your tongue or you'll be charged with blasphemy!"

After seeing priests enforce rules with physical and psychological abuse, Seth sorrowed. "Discipline like yours makes no sense to an Indian child," he tried to explain. "He does not understand why you beat him. He doesn't connect wetting his bed with being made to sit in a corner wrapped in a urine-soaked blanket!"

I'm not able to improve conditions here, and no longer can I stay and be part of these things, Seth told himself. I promised Father I'd find a way to help, but this is not the place.

Seth had become fond of Maria, an Indian girl who worked hard and tried to be cheerful. The nuns had shorn her hair to the scalp when they suspected her of an escape attempt. She confided in Seth when he offered friendship. "I don't have family," she told him. "My father drank. Killed my mother. My sisters died – pox. Whiteman took my brother – he didn't come back."

Seth's course of action became clear one morning when he came upon Maria as she peeled vegetables, tears on her cheeks.

"What is it?" he asked.

"I can't tell," she mumbled.

"You can tell me."

"The priest . . . he . . . he . . . I was mopping the floor in the class building. It was before supper – everyone was gone. The priest pushed me in a closet. He made me take off my clothes." Weeping, she added, "I was ashamed to come naked. He said priests do what's right with God. He touched me all over and put his hand on my mouth. He said he'd kill me if I made a noise. He did it then. I die now," she stammered, raising a knife.

"No, Maria! I'll help you!" With fury for the priest, Seth said, "It must not happen again. We'll leave . . . tonight!"

When a nun came into the kitchen, Seth pretended to check supplies. Later, he whispered to Maria, "Leave the window unlocked and slip out to the dock after everyone is asleep."

That night Seth hid a canoe under some branches and waited. He watched Maria creep through a window and flit through the shadows to the boat. Without a sound, he pushed off, and the two paddled the remainder of the night. At dawn they pulled into woods and hid until darkness returned. Seth had brought food but dared not make a fire. He guarded Maria as she tried to sleep. He could only imagine the full harm done to her.

The priests did not follow. They're glad to be rid of me,

Seth guessed, and they wouldn't chase just one convert. The next night, he rowed until he caught tides into Burrard Inlet.

Maria was bewildered. Though she was grateful to Seth, she considered him as a means of escape and trusted him only to a point; she flinched at his touch and misinterpreted his kindness.

"Seth! It's really you!" Stella cried, after he asked directions at Moodyville and found the Lees' house.

Seth hugged Stella, as Maria cowered behind him, barefoot and grubby. "This is my friend Maria," he said, looking at Stella meaningfully and seeing that she sensed Maria's distress.

Alone later with Peter and Stella, Seth told of residential school horrors and of Maria's dilemma. "I *must* do something," he said. "We need legislation to stop crime like that. I'll write articles like Father!"

"You should write, Seth, but the trouble is more than residential schools," cried Stella. "It's the changes in Indian life! Just imagine the shock of coming here from quiet Howe Sound to be suddenly surrounded by steam-powered saws, sailing ships, and commotion. Not to mention whiteman's ways! And churches cause much of the trouble!"

"Ay. Until the churches change, they're not for me!"

5

Peter tried to counsel Maria, and Stella talked to her.

"Now I'm afraid of all whiteman," Maria said to Stella.

"My dear, all men are not like that."

"I sinned. I made priest fall from grace and sinned more."

"*You* did not sin, Maria. It was the priest who sinned!"

"No, they taught me – *I* sinned."

Stella shook her head, despairing of the kind of thinking that Maria had absorbed. "Priests call that 'religious training!'" she raged later.

Maria began to function almost normally, though she cringed at closeness from Seth or Peter or if a man on the boardwalk greeted her with a pleasant *"Kla-how-ya."*

6

Seth worked at the mill while he made plans.

"I learned one thing right off," he told Peter. "Sue Moody does not allow drinking. And Stamp doesn't stock any in his mill store. Getting a drink has meant walking fifteen miles each way to a New Westminster pub. But now John Deighton, a Fraser River pilot, has opened the Globe Saloon, just beyond Stamp's Mill."

On a September day of 1867, Deighton had rowed through the Narrows. He had two chairs, two chickens, a dog, six dollars in his pocket, and a barrel of whiskey. He followed the south shore to a spot near some maple trees that the Indians called *Luck lucky* (beautiful grove of trees). He passed a round of drinks to mill workers, then shouted, "Build me a saloon and there'll be drinks for all!"

Deighton chortled as he watched the saloon rise in twenty-four hours. He climbed to the roof, hoisted a Union Jack, and began to speak. "Friends," he said, "you see here our illustrious flag. Let each of us think about what it means. To me it stands for everything good! It is the blood and guts of England in all her glory. The Union Jack has flown on every sea and has been my stalwart companion for lo these forty years. To this flag I pin my faith and to it I'll remain steadfast and true. Now, my friends, I thank you for your generous help. I will christen our saloon the Globe, and I'll make it a haven for all you loggers and millworkers. Your friendship will be my good fortune, and I . . ."

A rumble of conversation stirred in the crowd.

"His good fortune, indeed! Enough talk! More whiskey!"

"He's boring!"

"Too gassy!"

"Ay, Gassy Jack!"

The name stuck. From then on Deighton was "Gassy Jack," proprietor of the Globe Saloon, to which he later added hotel rooms. That corner became known as Maple Tree Square and the shacks around it as Gastown.

Later, Stamp left his mill, causing unemployment among millhands and loggers – and thereby diminishing income of the Globe Saloon! Noting prosperity at Moodyville, Gassy Jack decided to build a saloon on the north shore, and he pre-empted some waterfront property there. But he chose land regarded as the best canoe-beaching site on the mud flats; his claim was denied.

7

Stella had an easy delivery. The baby was a girl, Ida. Hugh Stewart, twenty-one by that time, commuted across the harbour to work at Hastings Mill, formerly Stamp's. "I tried for clerking at the post office," he said grimly, "but they wouldn't hire an Indian."

8

On the north shore Moodyville belched smoke and sawdust. The settlers incorporated and named the streets. Indians, bachelors, and beachcombers lived at the foot of the mountain on Canary Row and Maiden Lane. Most white families resided at Knob Hill from which a planked road turned down to the mill. Edging the dock were a school, a library, a forge, a general store, and a boarding-house – most built on piles above sawdust and mill refuse. Moody had side-by-side steam and water-powered mills. Hand-loggers homesteaded high in the hills, using skid roads and chutes for moving logs to the water. Seven ships could tie simultaneously at Moodyville's wharf.

9

"Peter," said Stella one day, "there's a Chinese man digging behind our house!"

"That's Wing Yee, a patient. He insisted on doing that as his *'mahsie'* – thankyou."

Wing Yee planted a vegetable garden and a strawberry bed. He dammed a stream for a pond, burned brush, and built himself a small hut. "Wing Yee stay, keep you neat," he said, smiling broadly. When a woman and boy joined him in the hut, he said, "Cousins." The "cousins" begged to do Stella's laundry and assumed other chores. Gradually Wing Yee and his family became invaluable help.

10

"It's time for me to leave Moodyville," Seth said to Stella.

"I understand. Where will you go?"

"I thought of salmon canning on the Fraser," Seth said. "But there's not much activity there since the capital moved to Victoria, so I'll go to Gastown – get work and do writing. I'm going today and have a look."

"I'll take an afternoon off and go with you," said Peter.

As they ferried to the south shore, Seth and Peter observed Gastown's row of businesses and small houses, all on pilings, that paralleled the waterfront. A boardwalk ran along the frontage, and a dirt road joined Gastown to Hastings Mill. Hogs snorted on the beach, rooting for clams and garbage, and cows munched on weeds. Indians straggled between the float and the village, lugging baskets of clams, fish, and vegetables. Farther down the beach, Indians, Kanakas, and Chinese huddled in a camp of tents and shacks.

They found seats at the Globe and ordered ale. "Lots of future here," said Seth. "Rough but interesting."

"I beg your pardon, gentlemen," interrupted a well-dressed man beside them. "I overheard you. I'm James Raymur, new owner of the mill. I plan improvements."

"I'm glad to hear that," replied Seth, "because I've decided to move here from Moody's."

"Wise move," said Raymur. "This mill's back to full employment and Gastown's doing well. The inlet is full of tugs towing brigs, sloops, and schooners – all loading spars, lumber, and shingles." He paused, then continued, "Forgive me, you're Indian but you don't look like a logger or longshoreman. So how would you like a position in my mill?"

Seth extended his hand. "I'd like that, sir. Give me a week to find land and put up a house!"

"Seth," said Peter, "I've made a decision, too. You know I have a lot here – what I kept of my pre-empt. I had it surveyed, but here it sits. Truth is, I prefer Moodyville – I feel part of it and Stella wants to stay. Gastown doesn't need me anyway – a doctor comes from New Westminster. So how about my lot?"

"Agreed!" Seth exclaimed without hesitation.

That evening, after Hugh came home, Seth said, "I'll tell you the real reason I want to move." He paced across the room. "I know we agree about what the church has done to Indians, yet you don't mind living here. But I'm not happy so near a reserve that insists on Catholicism. I've struggled with my conscience. I believe in teaching the love of God but not in destroying Indian culture! Most white do-gooders consider *any* Indian a heathen, you know!"

"Do you oppose Indians becoming Christians?" asked Peter.

"I do when they sacrifice everything meaningful! Priests make Christians but they make Christians without character!"

"I've said all along that the churches are ruining our people," said Stella.

"The government, too! It put us on reserves. Now, without batting an eye, the governor is making reserves even smaller!"

Seth paused, then added, "At least I've found an ally, a young Squamish man from Howe Sound. His name is Sahp-luk – Joe to mill people, and they call him 'Hyas Joe' to tell him from others named Joe. Hyas means 'powerful.' Anyway, Joe is Catholic, but with a difference."

"What kind of difference?"

"Well, he doesn't like restrictions at the reserve. He thinks his people were too meek when they gave in and became Catholic. We will get together after I move to Gastown. He's years younger, but we see things alike."

Then Seth turned his attention to the family. "Hugh, always be proud of your mixed blood. Your great-grandfather was one of the first white men to see this inlet when he sailed here with Captain Vancouver, and your great-grandmother was here to meet him. And Maria, you can be proud, too."

Maria jumped to her feet. "You saved me. I'm going with you!"

"No, Maria, you stay here. You don't have to . . ."

"I . . . I *want* to be with you!"

The family stared at Maria, surprised at her openness and at how attractive she had become. Her hair had grown black and glossy, and her dark eyes flashed above high cheekbones.

Seth realized that he had loved Maria for many weeks without letting himself acknowledge it. "Maria," he said, "you don't belong to me. You are free. You could go with me only as my wife."

"Ay! Wife!" Maria put her head on Seth's chest.

Seth hugged her. Perhaps she has recovered more than Peter thinks possible, he told himself.

The family chattered.

"I always pretend you're my sister, Maria," said Hugh.

"You are . . . my brother, Hugh."

"Yes," said Hugh. "And I'm not letting you steal all the family attention. I'm going to marry, too!"

"Hugh! Why haven't we known?" queried Stella.

"Because my girl lives on the reserve at Musqueam. I have lots to tell, and you may not approve. You see, I don't feel the way all of you do about reserves and Catholics. You get along with whiteman and live like him. But I feel Indian and I don't like people looking down on me because of it. I *am* Indian – Musqueam. My father was Musqueam. I want to live with them!"

"We both lost status when I married Peter!" cried Stella.

"The chief said I kept my status because I was born there."

"Your girl – what's her name?" asked Stella.

"Lay-yem. Her name means 'laughing,' but the priest changed it to Letty. And something else, my mother."

"Oh?"

"They call me a hereditary chief because I had a *sia'm* ancestor. Great Chief Luhk married my great-grandmother

Kah-te. Power passes through the maternal line. It doesn't matter that Kah-te was a slave because Luhk wiped that away."

"So will you keep on at the mill?"

"No, I'll try a cannery on the river. Uncle Seth, maybe I can help you fight at Musqueam. I *am* proud to be Indian."

"When will we meet Letty?" Stella asked.

"I'll bring her soon." Then Hugh picked up Ida and rocked her in his arms. "I'm going to miss you, little one," he said.

"You have a baby soon," said Maria, making everyone laugh.

11

Seth married Maria, took possession of Peter's lot, and with helpers put up a two-story house. He bought furniture, coal oil lamps, and a large kitchen range, which would double as a heater.

Maria was ecstatic with her new home. On the night she moved in, Seth closed the door and drew the curtains. Maria's lithe body aroused him. He removed his boots, shirt, and trousers.

Blushing a little, Maria unfastened her smock and slid it from her shoulders. Seth kissed her. Then he blew out the light and lay down. "I won't bother you, Maria," he said. "Not until you're ready."

Maria lowered herself beside Seth and thrust her body into his arms. She trembled, confused by the thrill of his touch and a blurred memory of the priest's attack.

Seth caressed her. "Are you sure you want me to. . . ."

"Yes . . . oh, yes . . . Please, I want . . ."

CHAPTER XXIII

Victoria and New Westminster editors suggested that after the United States purchased Alaska, it began to eye British Columbia; and that a movement for annexation to the United States was growing in British Columbia. Alarmed, Britain advocated: "Join the Dominion of Canada! Send delegates to Ottawa!"

The delegates travelled by train across the United States. They compromised: British Columbia would vote for Confederation if promised a railroad to the west coast.

In 1871 British Columbia became the sixth province of Canada and the railroad was approved. To celebrate, Gassy Jack held cockfights and raised a Dominion flag.

2

Maria delivered a son, Matthew, named for his great grandfather, but Peter advised her to avoid another pregnancy.

Stella delighted in a bathtub, a cooking range, a sink with a drain pipe, and, above all, mail from her family. One day, when she opened a letter from David, she read a few lines and shrieked, "Father's coming!"

On the day David arrived, Seth and Maria crossed to Moodyville with the baby; Amanda and Angus came from Victoria with their five-year-old twins; and Hugh came on the harbour ferry with Letty.

After the steamer edged into a slip at the dock, David bounded down the gangplank. At seventy-five he was balding with a grey beard and sideburns, but he was agile and healthy. Stella cried, "We wondered if you'd come back!"

"But this is where I belong! With everyone dear to me!"

The Lees' home on Knob Hill rang with merriment.

David enjoyed seeing Hugh and meeting his other grand-children: Ida Lee, Matthew Stewart, and the twins, Benjamin and Sallie McMechen.

"Louis is married and is in a thriving import business," David reported.

"And you? No wife?" asked Stella.

"That's why I stayed in London so long. There was someone, but she died recently. I'll stay here now."

"Back on the Fraser?"

"No, it's not the same. My memories are in Mahli and it's gone. I'll find a place here or in Gastown. I'll do articles or work with Seth on his campaign for Indian rights."

Stella tried to help Letty, who was ill at ease with the family. Her hair was in a braid, and she wore the garb of Indian women under church jurisdiction: a long plaid skirt with wide hemline bands, a dark tunic, heavy shoes, and a fringed shawl.

3

Seth pointed out some of his concerns to David. "Whiteman looked at our streams and saw only water power," he said. "Our forests just meant lumber to him. He even takes the measly dogfish to use as oil for his mills. And the reserve system is dreadful! At first we could roam and hunt, but gradually whiteman has forced us into smaller areas. We weren't able to stop him. We let him rob us because we didn't know what to do!"

"I argued with Governor Douglas about that," said David. "The government gives Queen's land to Indians, but it was Indian land to begin with!"

"And whiteman can claim land just by occupying it!"

"With no compensation for Indians?"

"Of course not, and it's illegal for Indians to seek

counsel. The new Indian Act abolishes native self-rule. I think it will weaken our hereditary structure to the point of collapse!"

David nodded, sharing Seth's outrage.

"I need you, Father," said Seth. "Everyone considers me as being completely Indian. I look and think Indian. Thanks to you, maybe I have enough education to work for treaties that will help my people."

"Don't forget that help for Indians is still my project, too. Perhaps together we can make ourselves heard."

"We're not fighting alone. I hear that Interior Indians are on the verge of war. And this province has fifty thousand Indians and only ten thousand whitemen!"

"At least this province has appointed a commissioner for Indian Affairs. You should have that position, Seth!"

Seth's face showed animation. "Sometimes I think about getting into politics. Maybe I could right some wrongs that way."

"Meanwhile," said Stella, entering the room, "Peter and I are taking Ida for some afternoon bathing at English Bay! We're going to ferry, then rent some bicycles. Who wants to come?"

4

Defying restrictions, some Indians secretly held pot-latches. Seth secured invitations for himself and David to one at Whoi Whoi (later, site of Lumbermens' Arch), where he introduced David to Hyas Joe. "My father understands us, Joe," he said.

Joe was talkative in his limited English and Chinook. Fingering his heavy black moustache, he said, "I'm a dock foreman now. They call me Capilano Joe, not Hyas Joe any more."

"Why?" Seth asked.

"Whiteman put the name Capilano on skookum-chuck [river] at Homulchesen, so I took name Capilano Joe. Then Oblates, they think I'm a good Catholic, so they send me there to Capilano Reserve and and tell me to make people join Catholics."

"Do you have a family, Joe?" asked David.

"My klootch [wife] Lay-hu-lette. She's a granddaughter of Paytsauma. Whiteman name her Mary Agnes Joe Capilano. I make home for my klootch. Make another home at Fraser skookum-chuck. I'm Musqueam way back."

"I was curious about the name Capilano," David said. "I learned that the Crown hydrographer renamed the Homulchesen River for Chief Ki-ap-a-la-no but anglicized the spelling."

5

At first, the Canadian Pacific Railroad planned to reach the west coast 120 miles north of Burrard Inlet, but eventually it chose a Fraser Canyon route with a terminus on the inlet.

Speculators watched land sales mushroom. Then engineers decided that the chosen harbour was too shallow and changed the terminus to Gastown, making it the new focus of land speculation and bargaining for rights-of-way. At the railroad's request, Gastown became Granville, renamed to honour the Colonial Secretary of State.

The CPR wooed labourers with wages of two dollars a day. To finance dynamiting tunnels it imported two thousand Chinese coolies, who dug and blasted for little more than their keep. Engineers celebrated with Tom and Jerrys when they reached Granville, and hacked a wagon trail through the bush to the chosen site of the station; that road became Granville Street. A census counted loggers and millworkers but excluded wives, children, Chinese, Indians, and prostitutes. Granville elected a mayor, laid out streets, built planked sidewalks over the mud, and pressed for water and sewage systems.

"The railroad grant bothers me," Seth said one day when he and David were walking behind the waterfront buildings.

"Granville has the terminus, but at what cost! The CPR grant is thousands of prime acres here on the inlet!"

"Hmm," replied David. "Is the CPR responsible for the rubble piled up here behind the main street?"

"Terrible sight, isn't it? Some is from logging, but most of it from the railroad."

"Another thing. I see Matthew – not in school again today, I gather. Are you worried about him, Seth?"

"Yes, I'm worried. I'm not close to him. There's a racial problem at school – he's snubbed because of being Indian. He goes to school at Hastings Mill but the teacher is white and so are most of the students. They call him a dumb Indian, so he takes that attitude and doesn't try. Father, we talk about what whiteman has done to the Indian, and here it is – personal – in our family, and I don't know how to fight it!"

6

Despite Peter's advice, Maria became pregnant again and had a second son, Robert, whom they called Bo. After the birth, Peter shook his head sadly. "Your little son has a deformed spine, and I suspect some brain damage. I'm sorry."

7

In the spring Granville workers burned the slash area behind the town. A smoky haze from smouldering fires almost hid the sun. Early summer was dry, and fumes from the fires hovered low.

On June 8th Granville was in a festive mood despite the odour. It was to be incorporated as the city of Vancouver! Anchored in the harbour with streamers waving from its masts, the *Robert Kerr* tolled its bell. Other ships whistled in response, and a band beat time as it marched along the boardwalk.

"Never mind the smoke! Let's celebrate!" said Seth.

"Holiday! Let's have a picnic!" cried Maria.

Seth laughed. "Good idea, if we can find a spot without mud." He hoisted Bo on his shoulders and turned to Matthew. "Will you come with us, son?" he asked. "No school today."

"Might as well. Wouldn't go to school anyway. I quit."

Seth was to remember that afternoon for many years. Except for concern about Matthew and some worrisome debts, he was happy. His position at the mill was secure, and he had interested some clergymen and legislators in his views. Several of his articles had appeared in newspapers.

At the picnic Maria said, "I'm going to have a baby again."

Seth could not conceal his dismay. Bo's affliction was a constant reminder of the danger. "You must rest all you can this time," he said. "We'll get someone to help with Bo."

"I'm fine. We'll have a girl, I hope."

The following Sunday, June 13th, was hot and muggy; the smoke formed a stationary low cloud. Seth, Maria, and both boys attended a service in the new Methodist Church.

After lunch, Seth said, "If you're all right, Maria, I'll take Matthew fishing in the inlet. Do you mind?"

"You go. Bo and I will nap. Bring a fish for supper!"

"How lucky I am to have you!" Seth replied, kissing Maria. He gathered some fishing gear, and he waved as he and Matthew shoved off the dock in their rowboat. He looked forward to being with Matthew.

Maria took Bo upstairs, put him into his small bed, and sang a lullaby until he was asleep. Then she went to the lower floor and lay on the chesterfield. Slightly nauseous, she, too, soon was asleep. She was unaware of the sudden breeze that relieved the humidity. She also was unaware that Bo had wakened and toddled noiselessly down the stairs and through the open door. He wandered to the side of the house and sat down to examine pebbles he found there.

A few children were at play, and most adults lounged on the boardwalk or in their doorways, enjoying Sunday afternoon leisure and the welcome breeze.

Behind the buildings the gentle zephyr all at once became a gust of wind and fanned smouldering fires into flames. The unusual wind rose to gale-force, and the flames flared out of control into a solid, blazing wall. Fire soared through the slash, jumped to tinder-dry tree tops, and attacked the frame buildings. The roaring blow was like an explosion! Houses, stores, saloons, hotels, and huts burst into flame; a church disappeared in half a minute; the entire town was ablaze!

"Fire, fire!" Shouts pierced the air. Pandemonium spread.

Maria roused to the din and was aware of being surrounded by fire. Flames licked the lower steps and she could see fire outside the window. "Bo!" she screamed, racing up the stairway to the room above. She could not see through the smoke and frantically groped for Bo's bed. "Bo! Bo!" Sobbing, she found the corner of the bed frame and reached forward as the floor collapsed, the windows blew out, the roof caved in over her, and the house disintegrated into flaming rubble.

Hysterical men and women ran outside, wailed for their children, and sped toward the water. Dogs barked, pigs and cows milled in confusion, and rats ran helter-skelter. The roar of wind and blaze thundered through the bedlam. Like lightning, one flash of fire consumed the boardwalk. Buildings collapsed as pilings gave way. In a shower of fiery brands and burning timbers, people leaped to the mud flats, where they grabbed rafts, canoes, and rowboats, or waded into the water.

Bo stared wonderingly; he scrambled to his feet and started to the boardwalk. A man whisked him from the fire.

"Mama!" Bo bellowed.

Lumberjacks crisscrossed boards, forming a raft, and pushed several persons into deep water. A pleasure boat maneuvered through falling sparks to take people to the *Robert Kerr.* Others propelled dinghies to the *Ark,* an abandoned cannery ship.

The fire was over in forty-five minutes. It moved more quickly than people could flee and levelled the new city of Vancouver to ashes, sparing only a hotel and the two-story general store at Hastings Mill, which became both hospital and morgue. An eerie, gaseous smell of burned flesh permeated the streets. At least twenty persons perished. Some people jumped into wells and died of suffocation, but most of the victims burned alive.

CHAPTER XXIV

At the Mission Reserve the Squamish and Oblates had rebuilt their church and consecrated it as Sacred Heart Church. On June 13th a special Whitsunday mass attracted a large congregation.

A boy ran in the entrance and shattered solemnity. "Fire!" he cried, pointing to the south shore.

The congregation rushed outside. Horrified, they saw a sheet of flames leaping one hundred feet high. Black smoke spiralled into the sky. Many at the church leaped into their dugouts to paddle across the inlet.

Seth and Matthew drifted in mid-channel with lines extended. Seth was ready to discuss Matthew's problems at school.

Matthew faced south. "Look, look!" he yelled, gesturing.

When he pivoted, Seth turned ashen. His whole world collapsed in that second. "Maria! Bo!" he roared.

Seth and Matthew dropped their poles and pulled frantically on the oars to shore. Their throats dry with fear, they battled the tide and the wash of many boats, rowed by persons either trying to escape or to help others. When Seth and Matthew reached the shallows, the fire had ebbed, but the embers were so hot that they could not go ashore. The waterfront was rubble. Seth stared aghast at the spot where his house had been; he saw only glowing ashes.

"Some are at the mill," called a man from a passing boat.

The road to the mill was impassable, covered with fiery fallen trees, so Seth and Matthew grabbed their oars and rowed.

Leaping ashore, Seth ran through the mill in a frenzy, his gaze hurtling from one glassy-eyed face to another. Maria was not there. In dread he searched a row of bodies, some burned beyond recognition. "The others! There must be more!" he cried.

"On the *Robert Kerr* and the *Ark!*"

They found strength to keep on. One stroke, two, hundreds more. They drew alongside the first ship and Seth pulled himself up to the deck on a rope. Again, one face, another, and another. And so it went: around the deck, and below. To the second ship. No Maria. No Bo. Seth moaned.

"Pa," said Matthew, "A man said some are at Deadman's Island."

"Yes, they *must* be there!"

"Lemme take you," said Capilano Joe, putting a comforting hand on Seth's shoulder. He had crossed from Capilano Reserve with other oarsmen in his long, sail-fitted canoe, filled it with people fleeing the fire, and was ready to push off.

Pressing his head between his hands, Seth slumped in the canoe with Matthew until Joe beached it at the island. There he saw more bodies and staggered through survivors. The CPR surgeon was bandaging victims with strips torn from their clothing. Still no sign of Maria.

Seth spied a small form huddled in a corner, head down, the little body wracked with sobs. A familiar form. "Bo!" he sputtered. It *was* Bo!

Bo saw Seth and scrambled into his arms.

"Mama, where's Mama?" Seth implored, but Bo could not answer or tell how he got to the island.

Joe pointed to a steamer heading for Moodyville. "Maybe your klootch is there," he said.

Once more the Indians filled the canoe with victims and people searching for relatives. When they docked at the Mission, Seth raced to the church and examined the crowd there. Then he let Joe take him and the boys to

Moodyville, where the ferry and another steamer were coming in.

Peter was on the wharf treating burn victims. Stella comforted survivors, who wandered helplessly, their bodies sooty and shoes charred.

"Maria! Have you seen her?" Seth implored.

Both shook their heads.

When Seth had to admit that Maria had perished in the fire, he wept openly. Then he comprehended that Matthew suffered equal grief. Not understanding, little Bo wailed.

Seth tried to console his sons, but Matthew pulled away. When Stella suggested going to her home, he nodded dazedly, lifted Bo, and followed her up the hill. Matthew trudged behind.

The next day, Seth went to the hospital in New Westminster to hunt for Maria. Then he examined the corpses at Hastings Mill. Hopelessly, he returned to Moodyville.

2

While wisps of smoke still snaked through the debris, the churches held a combined service for victims, many of whom had no identification and some, like Maria, who had been cremated without tangible remains. Some survivors clustered in tents; some remained on the *Ark;* and others camped at the False Creek bridge, fashioning shelters from blankets provided by churches.

Vancouver residents started to rebuild, it was said, before the ashes cooled. The day after the fire, a sign marked a tent as City Hall and four uniformed policemen reported for duty. A contractor started an outdoor restaurant with meals for twenty-five cents. When the Hastings

Mill exhausted its lumber supply, the Moody Mill sent more. Hotels reopened and newspapers published again. Grass, daisies, and blackberries sprouted from rubble, and north-shore Indians hawked produce. With donated supplies, two doctors opened a hospital in tents, and butchers imported beef at thirteen cents a pound. Weary of dead rats in their wells and of hauling fresh water, the city fathers finalized plans to pipe water from the Capilano River through mains on the inlet bed.

"I'm going back," Seth announced several weeks after the fire. "I've engaged a carpenter to rebuild my house."

"What about the boys?" asked Stella. "Matthew is so quiet he worries me. And you'll have to find someone to look after Bo."

"I know," said Seth. "Matthew is taking it very hard. As for Bo, I've hired a widow from the reservation. Her name is Jessie."

Listening to the conversation, David said, "I'd like to go with you, Seth. Would you have room for me?"

"Of course!" exclaimed Seth. "You'll be good for us!"

3

Matthew secured work at the CPR terminal but remained only for a few weeks. He constantly belittled Bo and argued with him. Several nights he came into the house noisily, and Seth knew he had been drinking.

Bo's retardation became more evident and his twisted spine caused a limp, but he had an appealing smile and was a gentle, affectionate child; he put implicit trust in Seth and seemed to have forgotten Maria. Seth developed a deep love for him, but he was so busy at the mill and so absorbed in his writing that he entrusted most of Bo's care to Jessie.

In time Seth came to regard Jessie almost as a wife, and occasionally shared his bed with her. Jessie provided for material needs of the family, but she did not understand white men's ways. Unfortunately, she failed to offer the motherly affection – and discipline – that both Matthew and Bo needed.

4

One evening David said, "Seth, we've talked of your going into politics – Director of Indian Affairs, maybe."

"I can't leave Bo. Besides, looking like a full-blooded Indian would ruin my chances."

"You'd be better qualified!"

"I don't think so. My own son has problems being Indian. Too personal for me."

David was silent and Seth continued, his voice sharp with emotion: "For years I've had to put up with remarks about my Siwash children. One time someone said, 'He may have white blood but he's just *Sitkum Siwash* [half-breed].' Once I used my fists when a man called Maria my squaw – as insulting to a woman as calling her a whore, you know. I'm angry. Most people are bigoted."

"We'll fight that."

"Something else happened today! The new manager at the mill fired all Chinese and Indian workers. Including me!"

David said, "Don't fret. There are other irons in the fire."

"*What* other irons?"

"I have a plan. Actually, I'm glad you've left the mill. Now you can speak freely."

"I don't see . . ."

"Let me finish," said David. "Here's my point. My

lecturing in England paid well, and an inheritance from my father has drawn interest for years. In other words, you needn't worry about money. I started working for Indians long ago and you're at it now. So let's get on with it together."

"Hmm," replied Seth dubiously. "What else can we do?"

"We can buy a local paper and editorialize as we see fit!"

The anger left Seth's face. "We'd probably have to start a new one," he said. "Both papers are anti-Indian and probably wouldn't sell to us."

"Then we *will* start a new one!"

Seth was enthusiastic. "Yes! With an aim to create understanding between races!"

5

Seth Stewart, editor of the weekly *South Shore Banner,* arranged delivery at every door of the first issue. He wrote:

The Indian and the white man don't comprehend the gully between them. For example, the Indian studies a dangerous situation before he moves, but the white man acts instantly. The Indian considers something accomplished when he agrees to do it and may postpone the actual deed; the white man can't accept that. The Indian doesn't understand that the white man will do almost anything for a profit. The Indian doesn't know that the white man often speaks many words to hide uneasiness. The Indian doesn't want the white man to interfere with his lifestyle, but the white man wants to be "his brother's keeper." Let's try to overcome some of our misunderstandings!

"Good article," commented David. "Any plans for the next issue?"

"Yes! We need to speak for the Chinese! Hundreds are

out of work now that the railroad is finished. I'm furious with the CPR."

"Why?"

"Because it brought most of them from China and from the California gold fields – just to get cheap labour – and now doesn't feel responsible for them! Do you know, Father, that the Knights of Labour are trying to make Vancouver a non-Chinese city? In their words: *'Drive out the almond-eyed Celestials!'* And why? So whiteman can have higher pay!"

"Does Victoria plan to keep the Chinese out?"

"Yes, with a fifty-cent daily wage! And an immigrant head tax of five hundred dollars. No offence to you, Father, but most original settlers were British and brought their sense of almighty Empire with them!" Seth's anger flared.

"What do you mean?"

"I mean that the British consider anyone inferior who is not pure white – and that means me, of course. I heard one Englishman say that the Chinese are 'unsanitary and evil.'"

David rustled through some papers beside him. "I'm a guilty Englishman, son," he said calmly, "but I'm on your side of the fence. I even can add to your argument. Just listen to this quote from Prime Minister Macdonald himself: *'It is not advantageous to the country that the Chinese should come and settle in Canada, producing a mongrel race and interfering with white labour.'*"

"Hmph!" Seth replied. "I'll add that to something similar he said about the Indians, which infuriated me: *'Natives are living on the benevolence and charity of the Canadian Parliament, and beggars should not be choosers!'*"

Church groups brightened a grim Christmas with toys, hampers, and dinners for "residents of every tent, shack, or new home, mattering not whether they are white, Indian, or Chinese."

Benevolence lasted only through the holiday, however; intercultural relations were no better. Seth wrote: *Racial animosity is as detrimental to this city as was our fire.*

The Vancouver Vigilance Committee responded with an ultimatum to the Chinese:

Due notice is hereby given, warning all Chinamen to move with all their chattels from within the City of Vancouver on or before the 15th day of June 1887, failing which all Chinamen found in the city . . . will be forcibly expelled therefrom and their goods and household effects consigned to either Coal Harbour or False Creek . . . furthermore, the authorities . . . are cautioned not to risk their lives in trying to rescue the Mongolians . . . as the undersigned are in terrible earnest.

6

Citizens were so aroused that they advanced the deportation date and raided a Chinese working camp. The mayor and chief of police watched while the mob hustled the Chinese to the wharf. The Chinese fled with their goods balanced on shoulder poles.

As the city bristled with racial tension, Seth and David persevered. They composed protest editorials for their paper and sent others to Victoria and Ottawa.

A black cross appeared on the building housing their press and another on the walk fronting Seth's house. Merchants refused to sell to Seth and David because they patronized the Chinese.

At a public meeting, civic leaders challenged: "So you want gambling and opium dens, spirits and devils? Do you want the city filled with pigtailed peasants who don't speak English and let their hogs roam the streets? Is that what you want in your neighbourhood?"

"It's lack of understanding," Seth answered. "The Chinese will adapt to our culture in time. White men were immigrants, too, you know. And the Chinese don't mind hard work. Besides, some are barbers, tailors, laundrymen – we need them. And many are learning English."

"But they take our jobs. We can't hope for higher wages as long as they compete!"

"Try understanding them and working as hard as they do!" Seth replied contemptuously.

On a February night, three hundred white merchants and working men marched *en masse* to a CPR Chinese worker camp; they forced some Chinese into the bush and tied others together by their pigtails, then dunked them in the inlet.

This time, when Seth and David condemned the attack in their paper, they were successful. The Provincial government reprimanded Vancouver for abuse of the workers by suspending the city charter for six weeks and enforcing martial law.

"Victoria sent a magistrate and thirty-five special constables!" exclaimed Seth. "Father, I truly believe our editorials accomplished this!"

"Would that we could do as much for the Indians!" David replied.

CHAPTER XXV

On May 23, 1887 Seth said, "The first transcontinental passenger train is coming today! I'm going to take Bo to see it come in! Father, come with us!"

"No, I'm feeling my age today. I'll rest while you're gone."

"Maybe I should ask Peter to come over . . ."

"I'll be fine. Just leave me a pot of tea," David replied.

Seth looked at his father intently, noting his deep wrinkles, the stoop to his body, and the shuffle in his gait. He left with misgiving.

The Fire Brigade and a six-piece band paraded. Two thousand spectators shouted, "Here she comes, here she comes!" when the train's whistle pierced the air. Chugging into the bunting bedecked station, Engine 374 sported blossoms, evergreens, and a portrait of the Queen on its smokestack.

Seth wrote in the *South Shore Banner:*

Vancouver's link with the East is complete, and Britain's shipping time to the Far East has been shortened by two weeks. From Vancouver, our Terminal City, the CPR plans to launch a White Empress steamship fleet to carry mail, freight, and passengers to the Orient. I predict it will be famous.

That summer the Federal government donated its Coal Harbour military reserve and other land to Vancouver for a park, which the city fathers named for Governor General Lord Stanley. While workers readied the park, a smallpox epidemic struck, and Seth found reason to agitate in the *South Shore Banner:*

The smallpox epidemic has affected construction of

Stanley Park with dire consequences! Many Indians living within bounds of the park have perished, and city workers have bustled survivors by barge to the Kitsilano Reserve at Snauq [False Creek]. *The city is denying the Indians their hereditary burial grounds because the sites are in the so-called Stanley Park, and it has forced them to use mass graves at Deadman's Island.*

Indian people have lived on that park land for centuries. They are entitled to their burial grounds!

Lumbermen damaged the land when they used native trails for skid roads. Now an ancient Indian path around the park has become the Sunday afternoon horse-and-buggy driveway. Park Road, it's called.

That's another thing! Workers dug calcined shells from the midden at Whoi Whoi to make Park Road pretty and white. But Indian skeletons are mixed with those shells! At Chaythoos [Prospect Point] *the road goes over the grave of Supple Jack, son of Chief Khat-sah-la-no, for whom Kitsilano Reserve is named. Supple Jack used to canoe every day from his farm to supply the Hastings Mill store with milk. Now the city has shot his cows and sent his ten-year-old son to the reserve!*

Almost all of Stanley Park has aboriginal significance. Indians believe that park trees shelter good persons' souls, brought there by birds from the Saghalie Tyee. In the middle of the park there's a stone that Indians call the "lure," and it's so sacred that they don't go near it. Rainmaker, they say, lives in a cave under the park; he opens the door to make rain and closes it to cause drought.

The city surely can use a beautiful park, but it needs to consider Indian traditions. Also to consider the deer, bears, cougars, and raccoons living there, the muskrats burrowing in the muskeg, and the beavers building dams!

2

Stella, Peter, and Ida joined Seth and Bo at a parade celebrating Dominion Day and the fiftieth year of Queen Victoria's reign. Leading the procession along Cordova Street were the New Westminster Rifles and a band with gold-braided jackets and gleaming tubas. The mayor rode in a horse-drawn cab; lesser dignitaries followed in a lumber wagon. The band played *God Save the Queen* and the *Hallelujah Chorus*.

"Let's toast the genius of all this, Sir John A. Macdonald. To the architect of Confederation!" cried Peter afterward.

"Sorry, I can't drink to that," replied Seth. "I challenged nasty remarks he made about the Chinese and the Indians." Then Seth smiled and added, "Forgive me, Peter. I'm easily aroused, you know."

"I understand. And I'm sorry your father couldn't come today."

"He didn't have enough energy. I wish you'd take a look at him. He's eighty-nine now and failing quickly."

"I'll go, too," said Stella. "I wrote an article for him."

A week later, David stayed home again when Seth went to the wharf to watch Catholic Indians form a flotilla and set out for a Fraser River mission. When Seth returned to his house, he discovered that David had died in an armchair, a copy of the current *South Shore Banner* in his hand, a pen and pad beside him.

3

Stella and Peter stayed with Seth until after the funeral. Amanda and Angus McMechen came from Victoria with Benjamin and Sallie. Hugh came from Musqueam.

Stella said, "I'm glad I visited Father last week after the parade. He was sweet that day. He called me Sehla. 'I like the summers best,' he said, 'because the wild geese are here, all the good spirits. It's almost time to fly south, Sehla.' I wasn't sure what he meant. Until now."

"I had a wonderful year with him," added Seth.

Stella pressed Seth's hand. Then she said, "I've brought something for all of you to see." She reached into her handbag, pulled out a small package, and carefully unwrapped it. In the palm of her hand she held the gold horseshoe.

"The charm!" cried Amanda. "Father showed it to me once."

"Yes, the gold horseshoe – he left it with me. I want you young people to look at it closely. See the initials *MCS:* Matthew Chamberlain Stewart. He was your great-grandfather, and he came into this inlet long before white-man settled here. He gave the horseshoe to your great-grandmother Kah-te. This charm links us to our heritage, and we must always cherish it."

The family decided to bury David near Sehla, whom he had never ceased to mourn. They took his body to the Musqueam Reserve on the Fraser River for Indian burial.

4

David's grandchildren commented that they rarely had occasion to be together. They plied one another with questions and spoke of future plans.

"Matthew, you haven't said a word," chattered Ida, holding Bo on her lap. "How old are you now?"

"Fourteen," Matthew mumbled, "but I don't have anything to tell you."

"Oh, come now. Maybe you'd like to travel or . . ."

"I'm too dumb," Matthew interrupted. He left the room.

Stunned, the others could see that he was troubled. They also were aware of a liquor aroma on his breath.

Then Hugh rose to leave and Stella said, "Don't go yet. "It's been so long since we've seen you. Tell us about Letty and your boys – and the new baby."

Hugh looked down. "Letty and the baby are fine," he said. Then he added loudly, "All right, you want to know, so I'll tell you! You were right, Mother – everything's changed at Musqueam! I went there hoping to help people as Uncle Seth asked. I know priests do what's right for us, but I worry about my family. Once we were happy, and now . . . now . . ."

"Go on, Hugh," Stella said kindly.

"It's my boys, since they've been at the residential school! The priest told Letty and me they should go, so we rowed them to St. Mary's. I remember how they cried when we left, and we didn't see them for almost a year. And when they came home for two weeks, they acted like strangers. They weren't the same."

"Did you find out why?"

"After a long time, our younger boy Charles told us."

"Can you repeat what he said?" asked Seth, vividly recalling his own experience at a residential school.

Hugh spoke rapidly. "Charles said that priests took down his pants and put him across a board to whip him when he said something in Halkomelem, and after that they shaved his head. They starved and strapped boys to punish them, or made them wear dresses. He said children were not allowed to ask questions, and it was prayer, prayer all day – before meals, at classes, and kneeling before bed."

"And your older boy, Johnny?" asked Stella.

Hugh winced and his voice was shrill with feeling.

"Johnny upsets me most. Charles said that priests get boys in the night and make them do bad things. One took Johnny from his bed, and he cried when he come back ! Johnny said he made the priest sin and Satan would get him if he told."

"Oh, Hugh, what a price you pay to live with our people!" said Stella. "Is it worth it? You know the white world – you don't have to live on the reserve. The church is robbing your children of trust and so many other valuable things. It's making them helpless! They deserve more!"

"Yes, it's worth it, bad as it is. I love our people and I won't leave. I'm mad, but Letty is a good Catholic. She trusts priests and nuns and makes the boys go back after holidays. Johnny says he hates his mother because she thinks priests are good like God. Letty won't admit that anything is bad and Johnny won't talk about it. We're not happy, but I tell myself that the priests will protect us."

"Protect you from what?" Stella sounded enraged.

"From evil. Priests say whiteman's world is evil."

"They've made abuse seem natural!" said Stella. "But I'm afraid there's evil in both worlds now."

"Those boys are growing up feeling worthless. They may never recover," said Peter. "I fear for them."

5

Greenery erased the devastation of the fire, and by 1900 twenty miles of graded streets and planked sidewalks fronted brick and stone banks, schools, stables, saloons, offices, stores, hotels, an opera house, and a two-story city hall. An electric street-car system extended across False Creek, and an interurban linked Vancouver and New Westminster. Holding six thousand acres, the CPR was the largest land promoter and developed status neighborhoods. The Hudson's Bay Company opened a store at Georgia and Granville, an "out-of-the-way location" across from the CPR's gabled Vancouver Hotel. Mission Reserve women paddled to Vancouver with eggs, berries, and rag rugs. The city profited from the Klondike gold boom by supplying ships and equipment to 40,000 prospectors.

On the north shore the Moodyville Mill shut down after Sue Moody died in a shipwreck. In the new Municipality of the District of North Vancouver the Squamish population decreased, but immigrants from America, Great Britain, and eastern Canada swelled census figures. Talk of an electric railroad in the Capilano canyon prompted one mill owner to build a nine-mile flume on high cliffs so that he could move logs to an inlet terminus. Seth editorialized:

Vancouver is a modern city in the midst of wilderness. Unfortunately, many persons still regard our Chinese as "yellow skinned vermin" and our Indians as "a dying race to be tolerated until it becomes extinct."

CHAPTER XXVI

Arthritis crippled Seth, and he lacked expertise as a businessman. Engrossed in his antiracial cause, he often overlooked financial details of his newspaper publishing, and he was unduly softhearted to anyone in need. He alienated merchants by accusing them of intolerance. As a result, his advertising sales dwindled and he was forced to defray expenses with his inheritance from David. Editing and publishing his paper without David became both physically and financially impossible.

I have no power to change conditions, Seth concluded. I'm more useful helping my sons cope with their problems – and doing what I can for my friend Joe.

2

In 1895 Chief Ki-ap-a-la-no's son Lahwa drowned while paddling across the Narrows. His daughter Tutamit had married without his consent, which made her ineligible to inherit his position. So Joe decided to claim Chief Ki-ap-a-la-no's title. He reasoned that his wife, a direct descendant of the Chief's half brother, was the nearest blood relative. Joe knew that the Roman Catholic Church regarded him as the leader at Capilano Reserve, but he longed to be more than an appointed chief; he wanted to qualify as an hereditary chief. So gradually he became Chief Capilano Joe and the self-appointed spokesman of his people.

Though Seth slowed his campaign to improve the plight of the Indians, Joe continued to agitate. At the turn of the century he travelled to Victoria and other coastal communities in a personal crusade. Indians, he argued, never had relinquished title to the acreage that the government classified as "Crown land." He wanted a treaty recognizing aboriginal titles for large reserves and compensation for so-called Crown claims outside the reserves. As he demanded more rights, he became increasingly unpopular. He failed in an attempt to plead his cause before the Imperial Privy Council, and newspaper editors began to groan when he approached them.

Joe explained his frustration to Seth. "My people are too weak. They take on too many whiteman ways. We have no treaty – the government just takes. Other provinces make treaties, but not here."

"We'll have a treaty some day. Then your people will remember how you worked for them. At least, you made some friends when the city laid water lines across the inlet and you took surveyors to the Capilano headwaters. And I see you have a story in *The Province!*"

"The editor promised a story so he'd be rid of me. I know whiteman now," Joe replied with a slight grin. "I know what he likes. I know newspaper men don't like Joe."

"They don't like me either," Seth added wryly. "The whole city is down on Indians. Whiteman makes us drunks, but he doesn't feel guilty. In fact, he doesn't try to tell drunks from good Indians. He just calls us all drunks – or half-breeds – and the police don't help us. But you know what I think, Joe? I think whiteman is afraid of us. He's afraid to let us have any power or own any land."

Seth was with Joe when one irate editor shouted, "You dirty Siwashes don't deserve rights! You'll get no more space in my paper!" Before he closed the door he added contemptuously, "Why don't you take your troubles to the King?"

"I'll go see the King," Joe said, not recognizing the editor's disdain. "King is hereditary chief, too. I'll tell him my trouble."

Seth grinned. "You'll get publicity if you do that!"

Joe invited Cowichan Chief Charlie Tsipey-mutt and Chief Bazel David of Bonaparte to accompany him, as well as his son Mathias Joe and Simon Pierre, an interpreter.

Chief Ki-ap-a-la-no's mother was Musqueam, and he grew up on the Fraser with Musqueam people when he lived with Luhk. His relatives there revered the sacred Capilano surname, and they loaned it to Joe for the trip. Chief Capilano Joe became Chief Joe Capilano, and he kept the borrowed name.

3

When Joe and his delegation boarded the *Imperial Limited* at the CPR station, a crowd of costumed Indians honoured them with speeches, band music, and emotional farewells. In London Joe and his group were a sensation as they walked the streets in full native fur, bead, and feather.

Lord Strathcona, the Canadian High Commissioner, presented each chief with a gold sovereign in a silver box decorated with a likeness of Queen Victoria. To each he also gave framed, autographed portraits of King Edward VII and Queen Alexandra. He was less generous, however, in dealing with important matters, giving only vague promises of citizenship for Indians and offering no definitive treaty arrangements. Though Lord Strathcona supposedly arranged an audience for Joe with King Edward, Joe never spoke of it.

Reporters squired Joe and his friends about London, but the London Express referred to them as the "Pathetic Pilgrims" and the "Red Indians." That same paper printed a speech Joe made but embellished the words, distorting the meaning:

. . . *White men are like a storm of locusts leaving the earth bare where they pass. They extinguished the buffalo,*

*and the moose is each year getting less and less. The caribou is
doomed, and our rivers have not the abundance of fish that
was the heritage of our forefathers. The closed season should
be more restrictive for the whites and more open to us. With
them fishing is recreation; with us it is our living. Our repre-
sentation to big chiefs of white race in Ottawa has not shown
effect, hence our visit to see our King Chief. Yesterday we saw
Lord High Commissioner Strathcona, a mighty chief himself.
We are sure of his sympathy.*

4

Another time, Joe went to Ottawa with twenty-five
Indians and gained an audience with Sir Wilfred Laurier,
to whom he declared: *"Sir James Douglas promised to return
our lands and fishing rights, but the government didn't keep
its promise."* Laurier pacified Joe with a pledge to discuss
the grievance with the Indian Department and the
Provincial government.

The press ridiculed the entire exploit. "Joe Capilano is
a nuisance," one Vancouver paper stated.

"You're all right, Joe," consoled Seth while the two men
chatted on Joe's verandah. "You have aroused whiteman. If
he weren't worried about the rights you demand, he
wouldn't bother to jeer at you."

Joe's comment was one he made often: "Lots of people
be glad to see me dead." He motioned for his daughter
Emma to serve them and said, "Whiteman thinks Indians
no good 'cause we drink whiskey. But I know whiteman
sells bad whiskey. Hastings Street, six bits. Man drinks bad
whiskey, gets drunk, then he's a bad man."

Seth nodded sympathetically, and Joe continued:
"Whiteman says potlatch is bad. I see whiteman dance at
Pender Hall – much worse. Rich Indian has potlatch, gives

many blankets and money so poor Indians have something. Whiteman gives girl present when she marries, but Indian gives to her parents. Blackrobes preach about Indian but don't know Indian. They hear but don't see. Whiteman doesn't know Indian. Whiteman looks at things from the other side of the mountain."

Seth repeated: "From the other side of the mountain. That's right!"

5

Stella gazed approvingly about her comfortable parlour, near the upper end of a steep dirt road called Lonsdale. Potted ferns embellished a plush settee and velvet-clothed tables. Gold fringed swags hung above damask draperies at the windows, and a patterned rug accented the hardwood floor. She went to the grand piano, which graced one corner, and idly tapped a key. We bought this for Ida to have lessons, she said to herself. And now Ida's in Ottawa, widowed and caring for the three children she adopted. How I wish she were here! I miss both Ida and Hugh!

Peter came in the room and kissed Stella's cheek as she smoothed her bustled skirt and sat with him at a marble-topped table by the window. Wing Yee's daughter served their lunch.

"Dearest," Stella said, focusing on the magnificent harbour view from the window, "if you ever retire, would you like to live in one of those fancy homes near Stanley Park? Or maybe Shaughnessy, where rich people play golf, join exclusive men's clubs, and the like?"

Peter laughed. "I have no wish to retire yet. I'm only a little past seventy, you know, a mere lad! Besides, Moodyville has been good to us and I still like it here."

"I'm glad you feel that way. Life wouldn't be normal for me away from the Indians. I live whiteman style, but I'm still a half-breed."

"A beautiful one, and only a quarter-breed." Peter looked at Stella lovingly. His ardour for her had not waned.

Stella smiled at Peter's compliment, then said, "Yes, I do like living this way, but I can't forget what whiteman has done to the Indians. I've tried to help Father and Seth, but see what's happened to all of us!"

"You're thinking of Hugh's family?"

"Yes, Hugh more than anyone. He gave up whiteman ties, and his family life is a shambles. But I'm also thinking of poor Seth. He's a defeated man now, Peter. Matthew has sunk to the bottom and Bo's problems seem worse."

"My dear," said Peter, reaching across the table to pat Stella's hand, "I didn't know Seth is that discouraged."

"I went to see him yesterday when I was in Vancouver shopping for a shirtwaist. Oh, Peter, he was all hunched up in his chair – his arthritis, you know – with papers he said were his memoirs. He wrote them for Matthew, he said, because he hopes Indians will win back their dignity and Matthew will be all right. Then he broke down."

"Broke down?"

"Yes, about Matthew."

"I've wondered about him. Tell me." Peter poured another cup of tea for each of them.

"Seth said Matthew went from one position to another after he dropped out of school, always losing out because he's Indian. First he worked for the CPR. Then he was a longshoreman, then it was construction, and so on. He was close to an Indian girl – Seth said her name is Flora and she's very nice – and seemed to be happy with her. And they had twins! Twins run in my family. My mother, you know, and Amanda."

"Did Matthew marry the girl?"

"I don't think so. He was drinking all along – the main reason foremen fired him, I'm sure. The last time he wasn't working, he drank himself into a stupor and deserted Flora, babies and all. Seth doesn't know where he is!"

Peter sighed. "I often wish I'd studied more psychiatry," he said, "because I can only guess at the reason for Matthew's insecurity. It's more than being Indian in a whiteman's world. I think Matthew – Bo, too – had unhappy childhoods after Maria's death because Seth couldn't fill the void in their lives. Matthew probably is terrified of being rejected if he shows love. Does that make any sense to you?"

"A little. It explains something Seth said about Bo. He adores Bo and can't understand why Matthew fights with him. Once he heard Bo say, 'I love you,' and Matthew laughed at him. Then Bo, who was only five or six, said, 'Why do you hate me?' Oh, that's so sad!" Stella brushed a tear from her cheek.

"It ties in. We'll talk about it again, because I must get back to my office. But what do you have there?"

Stella had reached into her pocket and pulled out the small gold horseshoe, which she had shown to the family at David's funeral. "My precious heirloom trinket," she replied, fondling it and turning it over to admire both sides. "I want to wear it around my neck. Yesterday I met a good jeweller who will make me a chain. So I'm ferrying over to Vancouver this afternoon. With so much trouble in the family, this means more than ever to me."

She put the charm back in the deep pocket of her serge skirt.

"That's a good idea," said Peter. He rose, hugged Stella, and left the house.

6

"Wing Yee," Stella called from the kitchen door, "tell your boy Kim to hitch Old Bess to my buggy and bring it to the front. I'll drive, but he can wait at the ferry for me."

I'll be glad to have our tramway, Stella added to herself, so I can ride up and down Lonsdale. She went to a mirror, pinned a hat on her pompadoured hair, put on a jacket, and gathered her gloves and parasol. She patted her skirt pocket to be sure the charm was still there and went out to the hitching rail.

"My," she said to Kim, who sat beside her, "I didn't know we had such a hard rain last night. It's so muddy! The ruts in the road are like gullies! Step carefully, Old Bess!"

One front leg of the horse sank into a mire-filled hole; she lost her balance and fell forward. The buggy tilted sideways, then overturned, tangling Stella in the reins and pinning her underneath. Stella's head struck a rock.

Kim leaped free of the wreckage. Several men ran to his aid, cut loose the writhing horse, and lifted the buggy to free Stella's lifeless body.

7

Peter was so distraught that he refused to face the reality of Stella's death until Ida arrived by train from Ottawa.

"I have to hurry back after the funeral, Father," Ida said. "My three little ones and the handicapped children I teach are my whole life now. My work is in Ottawa – I can't be here, too. You'll have to carry on alone. I'm sorry!"

Hugh offered Peter little more than sympathy, and Seth was far too disconsolate to help him. After several months of almost solitary grief, however, Peter resumed his practice and told Wing Yee's daughter to dispose of Stella's clothes. "It pains me to see them in the wardrobe," he said. "Keep what you want and give the rest to the Indian families on First Street. Stella would like that. She always helped the children there."

8

Bo went to school for a few years but could not keep up with his class. He preferred exploring treasures of the beach and woodlands. Occasionally, when he was older, he found work that he could do, despite his limitations; most employers were pleased with his uncomplicated personality and his willingness to perform menial tasks. Soon after Stella's death, he signed on a commercial fishing boat for a one-week salmon expedition.

Crew members of the fishing boat genuinely grieved when they told Seth that Bo had drowned. "He was on deck after most of us went to our bunks. He wanted to watch the stars – he did that on most clear nights. He knew the names of most of them, and we liked his funny stories about them – I think he made them up. Anyway, Bo shouted 'Man overboard!' and some of us rushed to him. One of the crew had jumped. We think it was suicide."

"And Bo?" Seth asked numbly.

"He went over the rail before we got to him or raised the alarm. We couldn't find him – or the man he tried to save. They both just disappeared in the sea."

Overcome with grief for Stella, with Matthew's plight, with his own sense of failure, and, finally, with the shock of Bo's death, Seth died soon afterward.

PART V

Hope

CHAPTER XXVII

Matthew continued to drink. During widespread unemployment that followed a financial depression in 1890 and a disastrous Fraser River flood, he occasionally joined lines at church soup kitchens with flood refugees and out-of-work loggers. Though he slept in missions a few times and tried to find work, he usually panhandled until he could buy cheap whiskey and escape his troubles in oblivion.

One spring morning, Matthew wakened in an alley where he had huddled under newspapers to sleep off drunkenness. Rubbing his aching body, he stumbled to his feet and slunk to the street where he hoped to beg money for more liquor. Anything, he thought, to blot out the pain in his head.

Squinting when the sun hit his bloodshot eyes, Matthew shuffled along the street and gazed in shop windows to avoid facing the bright light. Suddenly, he stopped, his whole being magnetized by something he saw in a window – something shiny, something familiar, something special. Surely not, he said to himself, but it is . . . the gold charm Aunt Stella showed us! Here, in this pawnshop! Matthew opened the shop door and edged inside.

"Get out!" shouted the owner. "No drunk Indians in here!"

"Please," begged Matthew. "I won't bother you. That horseshoe in the window. It . . . it came from . . . from my family. Please . . . how much is it and . . . and where did you get it . . ."

The pawnshop owner hesitated, ready to push Matthew out the door. But he sensed genuineness in Matthew's words and replied, "A lady brought it in. Said she found it in the pocket of a skirt she bought in a second-hand store.

Said she needed the money more than the charm."

Matthew drew himself up straighter as he listened. An emotion deep within guided him. "Please," he said again, "please, can you put it away, keep for me? I'll find work. I'll pay. I . . . I have to keep it in my family!"

"I'll give you two weeks," the pawnshop owner said. He took the charm from the window and locked it in a drawer.

"Thank you," said Matthew. Quietly closing the door behind him, he was wrapped in thought as he went down the street. He approached a sign: "Baths, 25 cents." He stood still, looking at the placard.

"Here's two bits if you'll use it for a bath instead of a bottle," said a passer-by.

Matthew smiled. It was as if the good luck of the charm were his already. "I will. Thank you, sir!"

After the bath Matthew went to the Salvation Army for a meal and glanced at the sky when he returned to the street. Above him he saw a flock of wild geese, and he recollected their being special to his grandfather David.

Matthew found work mopping floors at City Hospital. They won't fire me this time, he vowed. He rented a cheap room and carefully saved his wages. Keeping his word, he gave his savings to the pawnshop owner and paid the balance when he could. When he left the shop with the charm in his hand, he was jubilant.

Miraculously, Matthew never drank again. He returned to Flora, married her, and happily helped her raise their twin daughters. When he proved himself reliable at the hospital, he secured a raise and eventually became an orderly.

Peter told Matthew to keep the gold horseshoe. "Stella would be glad it helped you so much," he said. "She would wonder at the strange circumstance by which you found it. I never thought of whether I had seen her put the charm back in her pocket that day. The skirt went with her things when I gave them away." He paused, then said, "Matthew, I want to ask you something. About a theory of mine."

"What do you ask?"

"You really did love Bo, didn't you?"

"Of course. More than anyone. He was helpless, and I don't know why I was mean. Maybe I was ashamed of him, and that makes me ashamed of myself."

"You've grown up emotionally, Matthew. And you can make it up to Bo with love for your own children."

"I will, I will, Uncle Peter." Matthew straightened his shoulders in the manner of shedding a burden. Then he thought for a moment and said, "Do you know my father left some memoirs that he wrote specially for me?"

"Stella mentioned that. What are you going to do with them?"

"Well, I discovered I can write, too, even though I dropped out of school! I want to finish school and carry on where Father stopped. I wish he could know."

"I'm sure he does."

Fingering the charm, Matthew smiled and said, "In the memoirs Father mentioned that prediction of the ancient *A'lia* – that whiteman would make a black shadow of evil on the Indian."

"As black as the wing of the raven? I've heard of it."

"Right. I think the black shadow still lies on my people, but the little gold horseshoe has lifted it from *this* family!"

EPILOGUE

A speech by Tommy Matthew
Candidate for Bachelor of Arts degree in history,
class of '74

My grandfather, Matthew Stewart, worked for the doctors at Vancouver's old City Hospital. He also was a writer who campaigned for Indian rights. So had his father and grandfather before him. An English great-grandfather explored Burrard Inlet with Captain Vancouver. I have some whiteman blood, but I'm a proud Indian.

Yes, I'm proud, because my people's struggle has reached a turning point, a turning from countless defeats in the first part of this twentieth century. We Indians are shaking off our lethargy! We began to gain ground in 1969 when Pierre Trudeau, our new Prime Minister, stirred us to action. But not the kind of action he had in mind! Let me tell you about it.

Our people had tried to organize in the 1920's but encountered many obstacles. Indian agents were one; fearing for their jobs, they harassed our active leaders and called us rabble-rousers. They threatened us with punishment and curtailment of rations if we spoke out. Another obstacle was the Minister of Indian Affairs; he backed the agents' actions by supporting strict enforcement of the law. A major stumbling block was that most Indians were illiterate and could not respond to our leaders.

We influenced the Royal Commission of 1912-16 to adjust the land areas of a few reserves, but neither that Commission nor later ones dealt with our grievances. We could not pre-empt land, and we owned nothing; we could not vote, and we had no say in our children's education.

An imposed system ruled our reserves; our hereditary chiefs were powerless. At that time, whiteman puzzled us when he went off to fight in World War I after preaching the gospel of peace and taking away our weapons.

Two native leaders, Peter Kelly and Andy Paull, formed the Allied Indian Tribes of British Columbia. They persuaded Mackenzie King to send his Minister of the Interior to Vancouver in 1922 to discuss land claims, but the effort fizzled out. Later organizations – the Native Brotherhood of British Columbia and the rival North American Indian Brotherhood – met similar failure.

The Indian Affairs Branch divided tribes into "bands," classifying each Indian village within a reserve as a band. Then it amalgamated bands and tribes into councils and intertribal brotherhoods. In 1927 many Squamish bands merged into the Squamish Nation, setting up a council to direct their joint affairs.

The government patronized us and pushed us on to the reserves – for our protection and independence, officials told us. What a joke! By-laws that we enacted on the reserves were not binding until the government approved them. Alcohol and drug addiction, unemployment, prostitution, frequent imprisonment, and suicide became a way of life. Though the Indian agent on each reserve usually had a nice home, most of us lived in shacks without running water and knew only poverty, squalor, and debasement. Coast Salish culture and the Indian population fell to their lowest ebb. Our major concerns were fishing and hunting rights and the restrictions of the Indian Act. We also needed to convince the churches that native beliefs provided a sufficient standard of moral behaviour and that they did not conflict with the doctrines of Christianity.

During World War II we shook our heads in disbelief when the government banished Japanese Canadians to the

Interior. Our sons fought with the Canadian forces, but they came home to see white veterans receive the majority of jobs and educational advantages.

At mid-century we made progress. In 1949 we gained the British Columbia vote, the Dominion franchise a decade later. We achieved a revision of the Indian Act and once again were allowed to hold potlatches and engage in traditional spirit dancing. The atrocities of residential schools came to light, and the government terminated the office of Indian Agent. Whiteman also became aware of the damage that he had done to the environment, though he did little to improve such things as the pollution of Burrard Inlet or our deplorable living conditions. Governor George Wallace of Alabama, speaking in Toronto in 1964, said that the poverty and degradation on our reserves were ten times worse than those of Negroes in his state, and the laws governing us were no better!

As I mentioned, the major swing in our progress came in 1969: Prime Minister Trudeau's White Paper on Indian Policy. Remarkable things began to happen!

You see, Trudeau and his Indian Affairs Minister, Jean Chretien, promised what they called a Just Society, assimilating our people and making all Canadians equal. *Ha!* They proposed to abolish reserves, Indian treaties, and special status for natives. Well, Indians all over this country woke up and vehemently rejected such garbage. Equality must include preserving our distinct communities, not eliminating them!

Trudeau's plan spelled our ruination!

Protests recently reached the Supreme Court of Canada. A claim of British Columbia's Nisga'a Indians split the decision over aboriginal rights, forcing the Trudeau government to reverse its policy and allow land-claim negotiations. From now on a revolutionary Indian affairs program will include real dialogue and native involvement. The government is going to listen to us!

We Indians are beginning to assert our demands as we revive our traditions and take control of our affairs. Our young people are studying our languages and planning political activity. We are trying to restore our family life, which was seriously undermined by residential schools. We strive to overcome the stigma of being considered inferior. We hope to renew creativity and regain our hereditary methods of survival on the natural bounty of he land, which whiteman made inaccessible when he mechanized logging and fishing and tried to integrate us. Bands are pushing for treaties, aboriginal rights, and land entitlements. We are launching a rebirth!

Perhaps we never may fully recover our dignity and social identity. When we lost our culture, we became lost ourselves; we have a deep grievance and a heritage of bitterness. And perhaps the government will not keep its promises. Whiteman seems sincere, however, in his desire to atone for grave injustices inflicted on Indians for almost two centuries. He seems willing to restore Indian status and compensate for the lack of treaties in British Columbia.

We Indians have dreams, but being a whiteman is not one of them! Now that whiteman has stopped trying to make us white, he may realize that we, too, can contribute to progress. We can teach a way of living with the earth, not subduing it! I believe that Indian and whiteman can establish understanding. The last quarter of this century, from now until the year 2000, will be one of surprising change!

THE END

GLOSSARY OF INDIAN TERMS

A'lia . . . . .Prophet

Heisut . . . . .Celebration of womanhood

Iagoo . . . . .Story teller

Klanak . . . . .Feast

Kwakwaiyiset . . . . .Seeking guardian spirit

Mamathni . . . . .Men in house moving on water

Me'kwn . . . . .Cleansing ritual

Okwumuq . . . . .Village

Q'm . . . . .Leprosy

Shaman . . . . .Spiritual leader

Sia'm . . . . .Village leader

Si'la . . . . .Grandfather

Sinalke . . . . .Supreme deity

Siwcn . . . . .Power

Slalakum . . . . .Secret

Slowi . . . . .Pounded cedar bark, rolled into yarn

Smetla . . . . .Winter dancing season

Sqomten . . . . .Medicine man

Sulia . . . . .Guardian spirit

Sxwaixwe .A type of mask

Swi'wa . . . . .Eulachon

Syowen .Ancestral song

Tsawin . . . . .Coho salmon

Tsukai .Sockeye salmon

Whoi whoi . . . . .Mask

Also by Virginia Jones Harper:

Time Steals Softly is the story of Lydia Boggs Shepherd Cruger, a remarkable frontier woman whose longevity allowed her to witness American history from before the Revolutionary War to the end of the Civil War. Independent and aggressive, she helped tame wilderness and later became a wealthy plantation mistress and social leader, who entertained United States presidents in the nation's capital and at balls in her mansion. She shocked establishment in her modish dress, outspokenness, and participation in politics. The great statesman Henry Clay called her "the most womanly woman with the most unwomanly mind." History, love and intrigue create a fascinating slice of American life.

Order from:
DORRANCE PUBLISHING CO. INC.,
643 SMITHFIELD ST., PITTSBURGH, PA 15222
$16.95 (U.S.)